life of love ♡

Jane x

Daughters Ascending

by
Jane Dare

This book is a work of fiction. Names, characters, places, and incidents are either a product of the author's imagination or are used fictitiously. Any resemblance to actual people living or dead, events, or locales is entirely coincidental.

Copyright Jane Dare 2016

For Michael, Kez & Beth. Always xxx

But this time, for you too Loushi. I hope you love Carter.

"Let's take our hearts for a walk in the woods,
and listen
to the magic whispers of old trees."

"Courage doesn't always roar.
Sometimes courage is the quiet voice
at the end of the day saying,
I will try again tomorrow"

Chapter 1

Daron, a realm within Peith

Lilliana gagged as the fingers pushed down on her windpipe. They smelt of rotting leaves. Her eyes remained closed, as she slowly pushed her hand further under her pillow.

'A woman for leader.' The voice was gravelly, carried on a wave of fermented breath. 'It's an outrage.'

An alarm started to sound outside. Lilliana focussed on the methodical chime, as she swiftly wrapped her fingers around a tiny blade.

'Shall I kill you, little pretty? Or shall I steal a kiss first?' His voice spat against her ear.

Lilliana shivered, as the weight of the intruder slithered across her. With one elegant swing, she brought her hand down and drove the knife between his shoulders.

Blood oozed across silk sheets.

Lilliana gasped, recognising the slurp of a heart being pulled through ribs. It meant help had arrived.

'You're late,' she stated, slamming a fist on the bed, 'Get this man off me, Brennan.' Lilliana moved her hands to her hair, worried blood had soaked that far. 'How many more attacks must I endure?'

But it wasn't Brennan's voice that replied. 'Lady Lilliana, I apologise. I have only just arrived at the castle.'

Lilliana snapped her head towards the voice as the body rolled to the floor. It was forthright, confident, definitely from the northern territory.

'And you are?' she asked, narrowing her yellow eyes, wondering why Brennan had not arrived. If Lorcan insisted she had a babysitter, the least Brennan could do was turn up. She continued to stare at the man, now holding the intruder's heart in the palm of his hand, 'I'm waiting,' she said, moving from the bed and placing her hands on her hips.

'My name is Carter,' answered the man, bowing deeply, but keeping his eyes on Lilliana. A smile played on his mouth.

Lilliana pushed her shoulders back and inhaled deeply, driving the shudder of fear away. She would deal with that later, when she was alone.

'And what are you doing wandering the castle?' she retorted.

Carter bowed again, 'I saw the man enter through the window. Impetuous of me, I know, but I wanted to be of service.' As he straightened up, Carter raised one eyebrow and held her scowl. 'I can see I was not needed,' he said, looking briefly to the blade, still in the body slumped on the floor. 'I never doubted you for a worthy leader.'

The merest hint of triumph edged Lilliana's lips, and she allowed herself to blink.

'Thank you ... Carter,' she said, with practised grace, 'You certainly finished the job for me.' She eyed the heart filling his hand and noticed a spike through it. She followed the metal up Carter's wrist, realising the spike was part of a pewter wristband. 'That's an interesting weapon. Do you have much need for it?' she asked, stepping closer to Carter and running her fingers across the band. It was engraved with symbols from an ancient language no longer spoken in any of the realms she had visited.

'Not in your realm, My Lady,' replied Carter carefully, wondering if he should drop the heart, 'Or in mine,' he added, allowing himself to look at her narrowed eyes. 'But I have had reason, on many occasions, to protect myself. In my line of work, I have crossed paths with many killers.'

Carter paused, as Lilliana looked up at his pale blue eyes, though she didn't release his wrist, 'I believe you know them as, The Order?' he finished.

Lilliana's heart raced, 'You know of these people?' she asked, thinking of the possibilities from having someone in her close circle know details of The Order, and, what they might plan next. In the three months since she had killed her father, not a day passed when she didn't wonder at the Strangers who had blindly walked out to their deaths. So ill-equipped, but so determined. Her mouth twisted. It annoyed her that Brennan repeatedly warned her not to underestimate them.

As Carter was about to elaborate, Brennan burst through the door, blood trickling from his temple. 'Lilliana. Are you safe?' He halted, his eyes darting across the scene.

'Just as well I am, isn't it, Brennan?' taunted Lilliana. 'What took you so long?'

'I took a blow to the head.' Brennan looked at Carter now. Unusual for a Fae to have blonde hair, he thought. 'I do not believe we have met,' he stated formally.

'This is Carter,' interjected Lilliana, 'And actually, it was nice to have someone here, when I needed them.' She ambled over to where Brennan stood, her silk night robes wafting out behind her like mist.

'I apologise.' Brennan tightened his lips, thinking of the numerous times he had protected her since Lorcan had left, but his frown was directed towards Carter as he spoke.

Lilliana moved her hand down Brennan's face seductively. He raised his chin to meet her touch.

'Don't make a habit of it, solider,' she taunted, 'And find Carter somewhere nice to rest, before you clean yourself, and this mess, up.'

'You think it's wise to let this man stay in the castle? You know nothing about him.' Brennan's voice was edged with scorn and he knew he was pushing his luck.

'I think I can decide what is wise, and what is not, for myself.' Lilliana fixed Brennan with raised eyebrows.

He bowed curtly, and she saw him narrow his eyes towards Carter. This could be fun, she thought. There hadn't been much fun since Foster had left. She knew nothing could replace him, and she longed for his return, but in the mean time this would do.

'Oh, and Carter,' she called, as he turned to leave her room. 'Be sure to take dinner with us this evening, before the ball. We will make an occasion of it. I want to hear all about your prowess on the battle field with the Strangers.' She arranged herself in front of the mirror, her back to them, 'Perhaps my guard here, and his soldiers, could learn a thing or two.'

*

Blair, within the Caledonia Forests of Scotland

'You need a better plan, if you're serious about freeing more women.' As Toni spoke, she carried a tray with three glasses through from the kitchen. 'You can't just keep walking into the realms and not expect to get caught.'

'We can't stop now. Don't you see? Bringing home a few has given hope to others.' Sorcha was quick to snap at Toni. 'People are willing to help us, word is spreading.'

Toni took a deep breath, filling her mind with calm. She sprinkled freshly chopped mint and cucumber in the glasses. The liquid they contained fizzed excitedly, and then settled to a gentle swirl of bubbles.

'I didn't say you should stop,' replied Toni carefully, making eye contact with Sorcha, who was always so quick to bark. 'But I cannot make unlimited magic to buy you passage and freedom for everyone. There needs to be a new plan. A longer lasting solution.'

Ava didn't turn round to face her friends. She continued to stare out through the cottage window, beyond the trees. The mid morning glare made the view almost painful, so she squinted more and focused her search.

'So, our plan?' Sorcha interjected. Giving up was not an option. She was determined to keep rescuing Fae women, sold for marriages in neighbouring realms. 'If we cannot barter and bribe any longer, what is our next move?'

'Ava? Are you listening?' Toni stood behind Ava and

gently touched her arm. 'It won't be long before the consequences of so much magic, in one place, is felt. The Order won't leave this place alone for long.'

Toni's words swam around Ava's mind, as she paced to the front door. The eyes of the forest watched as she ignored both women and stomped out to the clearing beyond the cottage porch.

'You're driving me mad,' she shouted at the trees. 'If you're there, show yourself.' Ava yelled with more frustration than even she realised she was harbouring. In return, the trees bent to the breeze, a sweet lurching groan.

Toni was right. Ava knew that. The Order seemed to have retreated, but even Cedric had warned they were just reeling in shock. It had been hundreds of years since Fae had battled so publicly in front of humans. Long enough for the stories of their existence to pass as folklore to the generations that followed each other. Now, The Order had proof once again, they would simply be regrouping and wondering how to attack. Ava felt less human, as she wondered which side she would be on.

'I know you're watching me.' Ava's voice was goading. More creatures arrived to line the edge of the trees. Ava counted foxes alongside deer, squirrels descending from the pines, and, as she narrowed her eyes and focussed … two wolves. They crouched silently, never taking their eyes from her.

'Come out and face me!' Ava bellowed the words. The sensation of being watched had been growing for weeks.

Each day that had passed, she'd noticed the trees protecting the cottage, overwhelmed with deeper pinks and paler yellow.

Fear and anticipation sizzled through Ava's belly as she wondered who might step forward.

A voice wafted through her mind, as an icy wind rushed at her, blurring her vision. 'I am doing what you asked Ava. Do you not remember telling me I should knock? Or call ahead?'

Pulling the hair from her face, Ava watched Lorcan stride towards her, his long brown coat billowing open to reveal a torn shirt and bloodied chest.

*

Carter made his way across the dewy meadow, heading purposely for the tree that would grant his access to the Stranger's side. His strides only faltered by the gateway, trying to avoid battling turquoise lizards writhing in the moss.

'Perhaps it is too hot to battle today little creatures?' he remarked, as he entered the familiar shade and allowed the film of air to cover him.

As he stepped through the arch, into the Stranger's world,

Carter sighed and touched the stone work. He had spent so much time here and life could be so easy for him, if he let it.

'What is your business here?' The voice startled Carter. He gripped the arch as he took a step back.

'I came to deliver you some refreshments, soldier,' said Carter, smoothly recovering his composure and handing a pewter flask to the man. 'I was surprised when Lilliana told me she had guards positioned on this side.' The lies spilled from Carter without hesitation, 'Are we expecting imminent trouble from the Strangers?'

'Just a precaution,' answered the guard, warming to Carter as he tasted the sweet, syrupy alcohol on his lips. 'Not many of them find their way here.'

'Yes, but you can never be too careful,' came a voice from behind the trees. Carter and the guard both grabbed for the short swords hidden in their belts.

'Are we going to have trouble here, Stranger?' asked Carter, placing one leg further back to take a firmer stance. He watched the man open his jacket deliberately, showing them he had several weapons, confirming to Carter he was a member of The Order.

'It is too hot to battle today,' came the reply from the man, edging forward and shifting his gaze from Carter to the soldier.

A smile crawled over Carter's face as he remembered the

lizards, and, knowing that was his signal, with one flawless movement he caught his blade and sliced it through the Fae guard standing next to him.

Lilliana's soldier fell to the floor in a movement as silent and clean as the blade.

'It is never too hot for battle my friend,' said Carter, as he slapped the human on the arm and then bent down to retrieve his sword from the fallen Fae's bleeding chest.

*

Ava continued to stare at Lorcan. Wondering at his tatty, battered appearance, but incensed by his words.

'So you're telling me I was wrong to free those women. Women, who had no choice but be bullied into marriage?'

'Ava,' he glared, his intense stare drilling into her confused mind, 'I am trying to explain that there have been consequences. Did you think the sudden change in leadership would go unnoticed? Did you think potions and magic would be enough to quieten bruised egos and make ancient dictators bend to your will? A half Fae at that.'

Ava felt her blood burn and flood her face. She stifled the urge to hit him. She watched his dark eyes flinch as she realised she had raised her hand to slap him.

'I hate you,' she said, her mouth twisting as it resisted a desperate sob.

'Then use your anger wisely,' replied Lorcan, reluctantly letting go of the hand he had caught inches from his face, 'Because, they are not my words, or my opinions. They are the warning that a storm is coming.'

Lorcan stopped and pulled himself up straight, as if gathering strength. The wolves crept silently to his side, and he placed a hand on each. A slight smile formed on his mouth as he moved his fingers across their velvet ears, but Ava noticed his eyes stayed haunted. She wondered where the intimacy of their last meeting had gone. He had wished her well, set off to find Foster. There had been an unspoken closeness, a connection. She wanted to know what had happened in those three months, what had changed. She'd thought he would listen to her achievements, but he seemed hell bent on stopping her. The blood flushed her face again, raging this time.

'Why did you bother to come back, Lorcan?' Ava's voice was almost hysterical. 'You can't stop me,' she continued to speak, not allowing Lorcan any room to reply. 'I will talk to Lilliana, I will ask for an end to the consort souks.' Ava nodded fanatically at her own plan as she spoke. 'It served its purpose, now it has none. It should end.'

'Ah, yes,' replied Lorcan, crossing his arms. As he spoke the wind hurtled through the trees, dislodging a flurry of owls. 'How to make my sister see that being leader means listening to the ideas of others?'

'Who says it won't be her idea?' retorted Ava, snapping at Lorcan, but noticing fresh blood seeping through the white shirt. Desperate not to back down, Ava inhaled deeply, suffocating the urge to help him.

'I can see you need medical attention, so, if we're done here?' Ava answered her own question by turning and stomping back to the cottage without offering to get Toni.

Lorcan's body slumped once Ava was out of sight. He placed his hand over the oozing wound on his side. 'Yes. There was something else,' he whispered to the black wolf now nuzzled against his leg, 'I found Foster. And I found a way to bring Jess back for him … For him, and for Ava.'

Chapter 2

Cedric hummed softly to himself as he rotated his wrists, and watched the water slink from the bucket to the foot of the buddleia. It twisted elegantly as it rose to the call of his fingers. His lips hardly moved, but his heart sang as he felt the tingle of energy drawing the bees towards him. Toni often told him the long arches of flowers were out of control, but to Cedric it was a small piece of his old home. This was home now, his cottage in the Strangers world. Not even the sight of his old comrades, three short months ago, could make him mourn for the life he had turned his back on.

'And there was me believing you didn't use your magic any

longer, old friend.' The voice was smooth, but weary.

Cedric released the energy in his hand and straightened his back. It had been a long time since he had heard the voice, but the visit was not unexpected.

'For many years, that was the case,' he answered, without turning, keeping his voice steady, 'But, I'm sure you would agree, Heath, that times change. People continue to surprise us.'

'You judge me?' questioned Heath, stepping closer to Cedric's gate, but not intruding on his path. 'How exactly did I surprise you old man? By leaving? Or by coming back?'

Cedric turned and studied the man by his gate. The same piercing eyes and crumpled hair, both now weathered by loss.

A smile worked through Cedric's mouth, but didn't reach his eyes. 'I am curious perhaps, yes. But you, Heath, you know it is not my place to judge. I loved you, and Kallan, like sons, I wanted the best for you. I wanted all the power in the universe for you both. I have little time to judge others for what they have, or have not done.'

Heath noticed the chill filling Cedric's eyes as he spoke, memories of past deeds always threatening to tear through the peace. He knew he should show compassion, but his thirst for retaliation overwhelmed the moment. 'You loved us so much, you gave us the power to rip each other apart, and then ran away, leaving your own son believing you were dead.' Heath looked away. 'I judge you Cedric,' he said coldly.

'Why are you here, Heath?' asked Cedric, not rising to the bait of confrontation, but feeling the searing heat of the truth.

Heath didn't answer immediately. He looked at the neatness of the garden, the prettiness of the simple cottage. His heart lurched over with loss for Annie.

'Because,' he began, in a strangled voice, 'I need you to know, I thought they were dead. Foster and Ava. I truly believed them dead.' He rubbed at his face with one hand, scratching it absently, 'It is important to me that you know this. If I had believed them alive, well, perhaps I could have...'

'Changed their destiny?' interrupted Cedric, his face softening as he looked at the broken man in front of him.

'I watched them bury Annie,' Heath stepped on to the path now, seeking out the comfort of a smaller space, 'From the trees. As if I didn't belong by her side. She would have lived to be old, if she hadn't chosen to love me. I wanted to lie down in that grave with her.' He paused, the ache of grief grabbing his voice, 'But then I saw her, Ava. I wasn't sure at first. I watched how you looked after her Cedric, nurtured her. Thank you.'

Cedric stepped forward and put his hands to Heath's lined face, the way you would a son. 'She is capable. She has kindness. In time she will be an inspiring leader. She just doesn't believe it yet. You need not fear, or try and change her destiny Heath. She will do just fine on her own.' Cedric hardened his tone, 'You should leave her alone.'

After a wordless moment, Heath turned to leave.

'Where will you go now?' asked Cedric, watching Heath carefully.

'To thank the woman who saved me when Kallan left me for dead. It is time I paid my debts.'

'Atonia will not expect payment for her deeds, she has let go of many Fae ways.'

'No,' replied Heath, startled and glancing back at Cedric. 'It is not Atonia I seek out. She did indeed heal my wounds, but I owe my life to another.' He paused before he spoke again. 'It was Raisa who searched for me. Raisa who struggled with my broken body and delivered me to Atonia.'

'And Raisa that lied to your son and would have burnt him alive to serve her own goal.' Cedric's voice was taut, reeling with Heath's admission.

Cedric turned to face the buddleia. He shivered as a butterfly fell from a tubular flower. It lay dead on the path; wings crumpled like tin foil.

'Yes,' replied Heath calmly, 'I know that too old man. So I will be on my way.' And then he was gone. As abruptly as he had appeared.

*

Brennan watched Lilliana enter the palatial Daron dining room. The palest lilac flowers, nestled densely against gold beading, clinging from her neck to her thighs. Only the silk that cascaded from her legs to the floor, gave the impression of any dress at all. He admired the pride Lilliana took in her new position as leader. As he watched her glide towards him, it occurred to him that no one had mourned the loss of Kallan, other than the formalities they were obliged to observe.

'Why do you watch me?' whispered Lilliana, reaching Brennan and moving her face near to his. He inhaled the almond scent of her skin.

'Because, Lilli,' he always used her name carefully; she had given him permission, but he knew she was just as likely to rage at him, as smile, 'You look every inch the leader.'

'Is that the only reason?' she asked, pulling back slightly and fixing amber eyes resolutely on him.

Brennan thought about this while Lilliana stared. She had a new beauty about her. Her hair blazed red now and fell in fierce shiny curls across her shoulders. He wondered if she wanted him to kiss her, or if she was testing him.

'People will talk, My Lady,' was what he settled on, as he pulled his chair back and stood up, remembering he was the soldier and there to protect her.

Lilliana straightened her shoulders and inhaled sharply. 'And what will they say? That you are doing the job my brother asked you to do? Keeping me out of trouble.' She searched Brennan's face. 'You have done your duty, soldier,' she added, with a hint of sadness.

He stepped closer to her. Moving behind her, he pulled at a chair allowing her to sit down. 'I will always protect you,' he said softly, and she felt the words shiver down her neck.

'I've heard that from you before,' snapped a voice from the door, grabbing their attention.

Raisa paced across the room, dismissed the guards who had accompanied her, and seated herself at the far end of the marble table.

'If he whispers sweetly to you, he is probably about to betray you daughter,' she added, not looking directly at either of them.

'Mother,' started Lilliana, fully aware of the measures Brennan had taken to prevent Raisa being slaughtered in the chaos of the sacrifice, 'If not for Brennan, you would be dead now. How many times do we have to rake over his actions?'

'And how long will he keep me as his prisoner?'

'You are not a prisoner,' snapped Lilliana, growing tired of her mother's need for attention, 'I will allow you free passage about the realm when I believe you won't run straight to the Elders and plot my downfall.'

'Lilliana.' Raisa's eyes flashed the briefest gold, 'There are many things I wanted. Power. Victory. Adoration,' she glanced briefly to Brennan and then back, 'But your downfall, my child, is something I will never crave.'

Raisa smoothed the silk fabric of her skirt, 'But whatever you think of me at this moment, my opinion is still valid.'

'This again,' sighed Lilliana, knowing what her mother was about to say. She put down the crystal goblet she had been holding and looked at Brennan. She had grown accustomed to watching his reactions for the last three months.

'You can ignore me if you wish,' continued Raisa, wondering if her daughter had developed the same arrogance of her father. 'But the other realms will all have word of Kallan's death at your hands. Some will be inquisitive, to see how we fare with a female to lead us. Some will believe you are easy to attack. But all, all Lilliana, will feel the strangeness of something new. The strangeness of progress, the ignorance of which - breeds fear.'

'What do you suggest?' It was Brennan that asked the question of Raisa, but he didn't take his eyes from Lilliana.

'Marriage, ofcourse,' replied Raisa, 'Marriage is the only

option.'

The chair legs grinding against the polished floor, felt as shrill as Lilliana's voice. 'No,' she bellowed, 'I will marry when I choose it. And I may never choose it.'

Brennan stood up, blocking Lilliana's view of her mother with his body. 'I don't think she was suggesting you marry against your will,' he offered. 'Don't let her rile you,' he said quietly against her ear. 'She wants to make you angry with her. She wants to prove you are not ready to rule. Don't let her win.' As he spoke he gently touched Lilliana's arm, the merest pressure to try and make a connection.

'She would have me paraded at the consort souk for the highest princely bidder,' moaned Lilliana, looking into Brennan's face, focussing on his words.

'We can't have that.' The voice came from the open balcony. 'Surely the men must be brought to the castle, and paraded for our beautiful leader.'

Brennan released Lilliana's arm and drew a knife from the straps on his thigh.

'Weapons removed at the door,' he growled, moving steadily towards Carter.

'OK. OK,' said Carter, grinning. 'Although, technically, I didn't come via the door. But, I also didn't come to make any trouble. Remember, I was invited.' He looked at Lilliana and held a smile as he removed blades strapped to both legs and unbuckled the harness fastened around his back. Brennan noted it housed a series of ornate metal knives and pokers.

'And you are very welcome,' announced Lilliana, throwing Brennan a withering glance, breaking the fragile thread of understanding between them. 'Come and sit down, dinner is about to be served. I want to hear more about you.'

As the beginning of their meal was served, Brennan listened with growing disquiet as Carter began to weave a story of his early life in Daron, the son of a miner. Details that explained nothing, specifics that could never be disproved. He saw how Lilliana clung to the words. He wanted to interrupt, to question, to aggravate Carter into saying something tangible, but he held back.

'And so,' interjected Raisa, 'With such a taste for travel, why have you returned?'

Brennan glanced at Raisa. He wondered what game she was playing. She had played it for longer than most, he knew it would be subtle. Raisa knew she was being watched. It was when she felt at her finest.

'Because, I heard Kallan's daughter was your leader now,' replied Carter, sweeping his gaze across Raisa seductively. 'I knew it would be a place where history was made.'

'And you thought you would, what exactly?' prompted Raisa, enjoying the smile Carter radiated at her.

'I have no agenda,' answered Carter, without taking his eyes from Raisa's, 'I plan to be at your service. I wish to be whatever you need me to be.' The slow, deliberate words ran over Raisa.

Lilliana noticed her mother blush slightly under Carter's gaze. It infuriated her. 'I have a personal guard already,' she snapped, narrowing her eyes at Brennan, demanding he say something.

Brennan shook his head slowly. When would Lilliana learn the ways of her mother? How could she expect to be the great leader she needed to be, if her own family could manipulate her moods?

'Perhaps Carter could help find you a worthy partner to lead your realm alongside you?' Raisa threw the question to Lilliana, taking her by surprise.

'I already told you. There will be no marriage,' replied Lilliana, surprising Brennan this time with her calm, measured response as well as her immediate glance towards him as she spoke. 'Don't you agree, Brennan?'

'Yes,' he replied sincerely. He looked deliberately at Raisa, and then Carter, before returning his eyes to Lilliana, 'You are leader now. No one will choose for you.'

Raisa had seen enough for one night. 'I have finished eating. Send for the guard to take me to my chambers,' she squawked, and then turning to give her hand to Carter she remarked more graciously, 'It has been a pleasure to meet you, Carter. I hope our paths will cross again soon.'

'Yes,' he replied taking her hand and lifting it to his mouth.

He pressed a gentle kiss against her skin. 'Certainly we will meet again soon. I hope to stay here for a while.'

Raisa swished from the room, the midnight blue of her skirt dragging behind her, pausing only to tut loudly at the guest that had arrived chaperoned by more guards.

'Ava.' Brennan voiced his surprise, hurrying towards the door.

Ava ignored the glare of Raisa and entered the dining room. She smiled warmly at Brennan, who nodded his head in greeting to her. 'I think we are way past that bowing nonsense Brennan,' she said, laughing and wrapping her arms around him, planting a kiss triumphantly on his cheek.

'What a nice surprise,' said Lilliana, forcing the edges of her mouth to smile. 'I would invite you to dine, but I'm sure you are just passing through.'

'Actually, no,' replied Ava, ignoring the sarcasm and walking up to Lilliana. 'You have been so gracious, allowing Sorcha and I passage through to other realms,' she touched Lilliana's arm lightly, 'I'm here to thank you properly.'

Lilliana tried not to flinch at Ava's touch. Why was she so intent on being friendly? She had made it clear to Ava that saving Foster, did not make them friends. She didn't need Ava as a friend. In fact, if the leaders in the other realms found out Ava was sneaking around with her permission, it would be an invitation for trouble.

'So the rumours are true.' It was Carter who spoke next, stepping closer to Ava, as if to inspect her. 'The half Fae who liberates the women.' Carter offered his hand to Ava and waited.

Ava turned to look at Carter. His eyes were like cornflowers. Ava thought they looked steely and cold, but when he smiled, they warmed and looked almost vulnerable. It reminded her of Foster, and her heart lurched for a second. She finally extended her hand, but took Carter's in a firm shake rather than allow him to raise it to his mouth.

'You are gathering quite the status across the realms, Ava,' he said, watching her face carefully. 'Some don't believe you exist, while others look for you, to offer you refuge, or plead for your help. Your reputation is growing daily. But, you should be careful, there are some that offer a healthy sum to see you harmed.'

Lilliana stood clenching her fists. 'I told you I would allow you passage through this realm, tolerate you taking back one or two of the women that were important to you. I did not give you permission to turn this into a crusade.'

'What you describe was never my intention,' said Ava, addressing Carter, but noting the anger knotting Lilliana's mouth. 'I set out to help a friend, and right an injustice, not wrap myself in glory or fame.' Ava spoke firmly, quietly rejoicing in how certain she was of herself.

'What do you want, Ava?' Lilliana's voice barely held on to serene, and she looked at Brennan hoping he might have an answer. 'I have to address the Elders and noblemen from three neighbouring realms this evening, and you are holding me up.'

'My Lady,' interrupted Brennan. The way Carter studied Lilliana gave him concern, he wished she wasn't so transparent in front of someone she had just met.

'It's OK, Brennan,' replied Ava, stepping forward to touch the soldier briefly, but with affection, on the arm. 'I'll be quick.'

Lilliana sighed, loudly, and motioned to her maids to step forward. Each holding a different gown, they silently floated forward almost blocking Ava from view.

'My Lady, Lilliana,' began Ava, not in the least surprised by Lilliana's rudeness, 'I want to thank you for allowing me passage across your realm. For now though, the search is over. We have indeed, found and liberated many of your young women. Some have returned to their homes here in Daron, some had no family and wished to make a new life away from your world.' Ava saw Lilliana's eyes narrow, at the thought that anyone would want to leave, but she had prepared this speech and wouldn't be deterred. 'However, we will stop now. To continue, would jeopardise your authority and appear disrespectful. I want neither of those things. I hope to be welcome here in Daron.'

Lilliana's head shot up from gazing at a gown of purple feathers, its train alone would fill the balcony in the great hall.

'You! A half Fae, welcome here?'

Brennan thought he saw Carter flinch, but he dismissed it quickly.

'Yes,' stated Ava kindly, 'Half Fae. I would like to believe that both Foster, when he returns, and I, will be welcome.'

Lilliana lowered her eyes, and scanned the pale blue silk now being presented. Long thin sleeves that would waft past her wrists and down to the floor. She lingered on it, until she pushed the image of Foster's smile from her mind. She seemed to forget so easily that he was half Fae too.

'To that end,' continued Ava, 'I would like to tell you what I know from my travels. Information that could be useful to you.'

'Lilli,' interrupted Brennan, 'Perhaps we should ask Ava to speak to us privately?' He eyed Carter as he spoke.

'Yes,' said Lilliana quietly, after a pause, 'You are right. Carter, please excuse us.'

Carter paused, and then bowed to Lilliana, smiling gently, never taking his eyes away from her.

'But,' she added demurely, as he left the room, 'I do hope you will join me for the dancing later.'

Just like her mother, thought Ava, as she watched Carter turn and wink at them. When she looked at Brennan, she could see a darkness in his eyes. It reminded her of Lorcan, passion and secrecy igniting his face, and her heart ached.

'Get on with it, Ava.' Lilliana was watching her now.

'The leaders of the other realm believe you are weak Lilliana.'

'You cannot goad me, Ava.'

'I didn't say I think you're weak. Why don't you ever listen?' Ava reigned in her annoyance.

'Listen? What to you? I will never listen to you. I have advisers. I have the Elders.' Lilliana paused to look at Brennan, 'I have plenty of advice coming from all sides.'

'Fine. I will leave you then.' Ava spoke calmly. She silently prayed they wouldn't let her walk away. She hadn't finished what she needed to say.

'Lilli,' cautioned Brennan, rolling her name slowly, as you would a young child. Ava was surprised to see kindness dance from his eyes to his mouth. Lilliana smirked as Brennan raised one eyebrow.

'Continue,' said Lilliana, shrugging her shoulders and turning away.

'The other realms have never known a woman to lead before. They are waiting for your next move, believing you will make none. They talk amongst themselves and exclude you, because at best they believe you will flounder and seek their help, and at worst they plot to walk in and take your power.' Ava knew she had their attention now. All of what she said was true, but she had come with one aim in mind. 'I've heard people gossip and laugh about you as they walk through the consort souks, that your people mean nothing to you and you have no direction.'

When Ava finished speaking, no reply came from Lilliana. She walked the room and grabbed at a dress from the nearest maid. Ava moved towards the door, raising her hand to acknowledge Brennan's kind expression, as she left. Lilliana twisted the intricate web of lace around her fingers. She focussed on the glass beads sewn into the skirts and squeezed them until each popped deliciously, covering her hands in the water they contained. The liquid moved with purpose up Lilliana's arms as she muttered to herself, leaving traces of moisture across her shoulders and throat. Brennan watched her hair glow more furiously red, as the water reached the roots and sizzled ambition. He moved behind her and placed his hands on her shoulders, knowing that she could order him removed, or even executed for his behaviour. Instead Lilliana turned her head until her face almost touched his.

'Lilli, it is time. The people grow more restless. You cannot lead from the crowd.'

'I am ready,' she replied, but then, with more emotion than he had ever heard in her voice, she asked, 'How many times will I have to fight the same battle, before it is won?'

Chapter 3

Scanning the crowd across the Great Hall gave Ava a sense of exhilaration and drowning, melting together until she felt sick. Tucked to a corner, she touched the ruby petals skimming past her hips, and wondered at how she was now part of this world. Fear rippled through her stomach at the thought she had influenced Lilliana, and collided with the excitement that she might belong here some day. Invited to every dance, every state occasion in the realm of Daron. A deep shiver lingered against her back.

'Don't say a word.' The voice was low, iced with longing. She hoped she hadn't imagined it, almost as much as she didn't want it to be him.

'Lorcan,' she muttered, shivering. The air between them thickened, drawing him closer. His dishevelled appearance had been replaced with a jacket fitted tightly to his body and Ava could smell mint on his skin as she leaned closer to him.

'You look...,' he stumbled over the words, but kept his eyes fixed on her, 'You look, as if you belong here.'

Ava watched his eyes move across her, and despite the thrill of his intimacy, she wanted to pick at him.

'Is that your way of apologising?' she asked rigidly. She smoothed at the skirt again, noticing the corners of his mouth twitch at her edgy tone.

'Come with me.' he stated, grabbing her hand and squeezing her fingers harder than she felt necessary. 'It is important we speak. And we may never have this time again.'

The words lingered as a sense of dread built in her chest. She looked directly at him now, sought out his inky eyes and prepared to lose herself in them.

'OK,' she said, so quietly she doubted he heard it. She wondered if she should say it again, louder, but Lorcan was already pulling her away from the crowd with such intensity a flurry of petals still danced in her place.

*

Lilliana watched the crowd below her. Hidden from their view, she pulled at the scorching red ringlet nestled near her ear. In just a few seconds she would walk out on a balcony she had stood on a thousand times. The crowd would notice, and the whoosh of dancing would stop, the throbbing drum beat would cease, the flock of colours would no longer meld together but be perfectly still, like jewels on a crystal canvas. And they would all stare at her. She turned to look, one last time, in the mirror that covered the wall behind her. Her hair, piled high like her mother, looked ready to topple. Her eyes, hard like her father's, betrayed the fear contained in every muscle of her face. As she took two steps forward, a blaze of steam shot across the great hall and silence fell. Lilliana scanned the crowd for Brennan. He stood tall, just below her and bowed his head deeply, only raising his eyes briefly to throw her some courage. Here she was, leader of Daron. She took the deepest breath. She had what she'd always wanted and now … she just had to figure out how to keep it.

*

Carter gazed at Lilliana as she allowed the cheers and applause to wash over her. She certainly was to be admired, he thought. He tapped his fingers impatiently against a stream of water flowing from the pale marble wall, interrupting its flow towards the glass pools framing the dance floor.

'Careful, Carter. I didn't have you down as so easily distracted.'

Carter swung round, touching his fingers to the levers connected to his palm.

'Perhaps it is you that needs to be careful, Heath,' hissed Carter, trying to regain a smile, 'Sneaking up on a man this heavily armed could be dangerous.'

'She has grown to be strong and beautiful. Do you believe she could love you?'

Carter considered the question. And decided to change the subject.

'Do we have a deal? Yes or No?'

'Always in such a hurry young one.' Heath raised a weak smile that crinkled around his eyes. 'What do you think makes this world go round, boy?' He placed his hands in the pockets of his long coat and sighed wearily, 'I used to believe that the most beautiful things in this world could not be seen or touched, they had to be felt. But I was a fool, and I lost everything. War. War is what the worlds are made of. It makes economies. It makes people belong. Every species, every day, fighting and trusting no one. We are, each of us, always one step away from wanting to kill the next man.'

Carter moved nervously towards the shadows. He could hear Lilliana preaching to the crowd. He wanted to listen. He felt drawn to her voice, so he needed to conclude this business quickly.

'I do not believe we met by chance,' Carter stood tall, 'I believe it was destined. You want your power back, a way to harness all the realms and make them bow to you. But I know you are a man of honour, and I know you want to bring Foster and Ava to your side.' Carter was in full flow now, practised and poised. 'I can make that happen. I have the sorcery, to make a weapon, giving you what you want and more. I can give your children something they dearly want, making you a hero in their eyes. All you need is the amulet Kallan's widow keeps, and me.'

'Remind me, Carter,' said Heath carefully, 'Why would you want to help me?'

'I won't pretend there is no price,' smiled Carter, 'I am ambitious, I have floated far too long. So, I ask for the highest rank as your advisor and leader of your armies.'

'And what of her? What happens to Lilliana?' asked Heath, noticing the increasing glances towards the balcony.

Carter stayed silent. He had no answer. He had not factored Lilliana into any plans he had.

'I will give you my answer when I have found Raisa.' Heath spoke bluntly. His voice seemed to linger even when Carter could no longer see him.

Carter stepped out of the shadows, his eyes drawn to the balcony and the wildness of the young woman who stood there, arms raised and voice strong. His heart raced for a way to amend the plan, a way to keep her safe. But just as quickly, his ambition crushed the new feelings. Anger and disorder twisted his thoughts as he moved forward, desperately trying to regain his usual brashness.

'My apologies,' said an elegantly dressed guard, accidentally clipping the side of Carter as they passed.

'Apology accepted,' replied Carter, swinging round and driving his dagger between the guard's shoulders, 'Just don't let it happen again', he muttered, as he twisted the blade until he felt the heart split in two.

*

On the balcony, Lilliana was nearly finished. The people of Daron had applauded, and with each wave of chanting, she felt the bite of fear grow smaller.

'Death is many things,' she shouted out into the crowd, 'Including, the start of something new. For too long we have been thankful that we still exist. Watching, as our magic flows away weak and useless. But every day is a new beginning, and tomorrow will be no different.'

Silence fell over the room. Noblemen and guards from

other realms started to move forward, eager to hear if the young woman they had come to measure up would say something of interest to them.

'I will restore power to this realm, and all the realms around us. The Strangers will come to cherish us. We will make them gaze in wonder. We will make them crave our magic and we will grow strong and glorious.'

Lilliana raised her hands, the way her father had always done, and felt the water from the pools below weave up through the air to meet her fingers. She let the coolness cover her.

'And how do you propose to do this, female?' The voice was sharp and came from a large, elderly Fae wearing robes common in one of realms that held consort souks.

Lilliana held her gaze, her eyes burned yellow against his sneer.

'We will take a deep breath and start again. We have lived a long time and nothing will keep us from majesty and greatness. We will remember our life makes all other miracles possible.' Her voice was rising to a roar. 'We need to move through the pain and clear a path for a new dawn. A dawn where we concentrate on healing Daron. A new day, where we seek better counsel and respect the people of our own land. We are Daron, together, and we will not stay broken.'

'You talk in riddles, like your father, but have none of his strength. You won't last beyond five moons.' It was a skinnier Fae this time, waving a stick crusted with jewels.

Lilliana took a deep breath. She had been waiting for this moment. Waiting to answer all her critics.

'At the centre of my being I have the answer, I know who I am and I know what I want. I live for Daron and I will restore our fertility first, and our power. It starts now … with my first law as leader. From this day forward there is no purpose for our women to be sold at souks. That time has passed.'

The crowd erupted. Lilliana could hear her name being chanted, but she could see the angry faces gathering below her balcony. She watched her own people cry with joy, as Brennan's guards rushed forward to calm the leaders of the other realms, now clamouring towards the crumpled marble steps twisting towards the balcony.

In one final gesture she stretched out her fingers and stabbed at the air. As droplets of water hurled themselves from the pools, surrounding her in an envelope of water, she yelled,

'From this moment, no female will ever be sold again. Daron will not do business that diminishes its own power and the value of its people. This is my word.'

*

'Where are we?' Ava's voice became a breathy whisper as she drank in the small walled garden. It was impossible to tell if they were inside, or outside the castle. The sky was painted the darkest grape, but she could feel a warm dew against her skin. The thick trunk of an ancient tree spread its branches like a hand, and invited her to move under its cover.

Lorcan didn't speak, but she could feel him close to her. It had been that way since they'd left the Great Hall, but she couldn't remember the walk to reach this room. Lorcan's hand reached towards the tree and droplets of water ran along his fingers, weaving down his wrist. For the first time, Ava noticed small white scars searing his knuckles and black ink marks across his wrist, identical to those she had seen on his back months earlier. Marks of power, of water and energy. Lilliana had called them the marks of his majesty, recalled Ava. Lorcan watched the water, studied it with admiration and respect, and with each second that passed a lantern shone to life. Ava stood captivated, as the tree blossomed with warm amber light.

'Where did you go?' asked Ava slowly. Her voice was taut, but she wanted to know why he was behaving as if they'd shared nothing.

'That is for another time,' he answered. His voice was distant but firm, and it reminded her of the first time she had met him, at the party in Blair.

'It's beautiful,' replied Ava, reaching out to touch one of the lanterns. Her heart was racing. She felt connected to the tree, as if she somehow had a part in making it so breathtaking.

'The light is delicate,' cautioned Lorcan gently. As he spoke he caught her fingers in his own and placed them gently together at the back of a sphere of light.

Ava's stomach shivered. She closed her eyes, letting Lorcan's hand guide her own across the smooth, liquid surface of the light. 'What are they made of?' Her voice struggled to find calm and she was surprised the words reached the surface.

'Like everything here. It draws power from understanding the Universe.'

'More riddles,' said Ava, feeling a new impatience rise quickly through her chest. 'When will you start to trust me?' Cutting short anything further she might add, her body jolted as Lorcan pulled her towards him, removing the small space keeping her composure intact.

'You are not invincible,' he whispered curtly against her cheek. He smelt of leather and peppermint.

'I know that,' hissed Ava. She felt his lashes brush down her cheek. 'But I am not the girl you met all those months ago.'

Hundreds of lights now glowed a deep amber, highlighting every line and crevice of the tree. Small spheres broke away and floated slowly from the branches. Some were already so high, the darkness above looked punctured by thousands of far away stars.

'I don't doubt the power and kindness within you.' Lorcan's voice was tight, almost unkind, but it sizzled down her spine. 'But it is no match for the intolerance and hatred I have seen. The very men you seek to deprive of slaves, possess enough wealth to pay for your slaughter many times over. Do you think they would hesitate to slice you open and hold up your heart as a trophy?'

'So what do you suggest I do?' raged Ava, pulling back, but immediately feeling the loss of his heart beat. 'What could possibly be more important than stopping the consort souks?' Her stare was soaked with resentment.

Lorcan lowered his gaze. 'I found Foster,' he said simply.

'What?' Ava was stunned. She forgot herself and stepped back towards Lorcan. She would have thrown her arms around him, but he stood still. Slowly, darkly, his gaze came up to meet hers. 'He is alive? Isn't he?' The words scratched at Ava's mouth as she contemplated what he might say next.

'Yes.'

'Can I see him?' Ava had so many questions her mouth couldn't co-ordinate with her brain, but Lorcan didn't give her time to speak. He ignored her and the darkness in his eyes spread across his face.

The light surrounding them faded rapidly until all Ava could see was Lorcan. The tension in the small space between them was solid, linking their bodies.

'All that is important right now is that Foster and I met a man. A Fae. He told us an ancient story. A story of a human girl, hundreds of years ago, who gave her life to help the Fae.' Ava watched Lorcan's mouth as he spoke. She watched his lips move in a different rhythm to the words, and remembered how they had felt against her mouth. 'He reminded us that everything has a price,' continued Lorcan, 'Those Fae were grateful and created a spell to return the human to her family – alive. So you see, Foster will come home. He will come home because together, Carter will show us how to bring Jess back.'

'Wait,' Ava's stomach lurched, 'Bring her back? That's not possible. I saw her die!' Her heart raced, making it impossible to breathe. 'Who told you this? Did you say Carter?'

'Yes, the man we met. Carter. He is not from the realm of Daron.' Lorcan studied her face, looking for the joy he had expected to see. 'Ava, if this is to work you must promise me you won't talk to Lilliana yet. We need calm in the other realms. To attempt such sorcery, while under threat from spies and armies would be reckless.'

'Reckless?' Ava lifted her chin and laughed, 'You think I'm reckless? After what you just told me?'

Lorcan stood motionless. He could feel her breath as she raged. The heat of her words ran over him. She had no idea how much he wanted her, and it stabbed at him that he would never be enough.

'Don't you want Jess back?' he asked, confused and reaching to touch the tears staining Ava's cheek.

'She is dead,' screamed Ava, flinching at the passion in his touch, 'She is dead. And you are not a God.' She sobbed, the words heavy as they fell from her lips.

There was no space between them as Lorcan placed his hands flat against Ava's cheeks, holding her face as her body wilted. In another world, he would have kissed her now, but the moment was lost as she fired bitter words at him, 'It's too late. I've already planted the seed in Lilliana's mind. If I get my own way, the consort souks will end tonight.'

The room fell into total darkness.

'Ava,' whispered Lorcan, his fingers reaching into her hair, 'If that is true, then you need to find safety. I fear there will be blood shed before the dawn comes.'

Ava let the words flutter down her back. She tried to process what he was saying as his breath seared her forehead.

'My Lord. I'm sorry to interrupt.'

Both Ava and Lorcan jumped apart at the sound of Brennan's voice.

'I know you said no one was to disturb you,' Brennan pulled the door open, determined to make a point, 'But, the

Great Hall has become a battle ground. Lilliana commands your presence.'

Chapter 4

Ava shivered through a million goosebumps, watching the Fae cram into the Great Hall. Shoulder to shoulder, they raised their hands and chanted. The beauty of the sound, celestial and piercing, was broken only by the line of Elders pumping their fists to a beating base. Ava watched the effort on the faces around her increase, until a cold mist made her focus on the floor. It was awash with foam, and as the bubbles rose, tiny silvery creatures flew towards the raised hands of Daron.

'Asrai,' whispered Lorcan, only looking away from them briefly, to acknowledge Ava's confusion. 'Remember, I told you about them when we passed through to The Forest of the Sith.'

Ava burnt, remembering the night in the tree house. The night she and Lorcan had kissed.

'Put your hands up,' he instructed curtly.

'What?'

'Just do it, copy me, and concentrate on helping the Asrai to rise.'

Ava did what she was told. She hated Lorcan bossing her about, but in the absence of anything else, she raised her hands. She listened to the music coming from the Fae, allowed it to melt over her. Then she remembered. The Asrai, small, female Fae, who melt away into a pool of water when captured or exposed to sunlight. The people of Daron were calling them to rise. Ava watched stunned as the room darkened, and, one by one, elegant, translucent creatures weaved their way out of the foaming water and bounced off the hands of the Fae. She felt a strange tingle through her body as she became one with the wave of hands, a launching post for these beautiful creatures. They felt fluid, emollient, and every now and again Ava was sure she felt a sting. And then there was screaming. Through the bank of water just beyond her hands she could see the leaders of the other realms drop their blades. She watched them cover their faces and writhe as if acid had been thrown at them. As more and more Asrai wrapped themselves around Fae from other realms, it became clear to Ava that Daron had an unlikely, but deadly ally, and she wondered what the Fae of Daron could possibly have done to warrant such protection.

*

'I will not back down, brother.'

Lilliana surged into the dining room, after Lorcan, banging her firsts on the table, as she looked for support. The battle in the Great Hall was finished, everyone looked soaked and exhausted.

'You cannot come back, unannounced and overturn my decisions. I will not be your puppet.' Her words were loud and edged with rage. Hair fell like waves of fire around her shoulders and seemed to climb and fall as her voice tumbled from her.

'I didn't ask you to back down, Lilli,' replied Lorcan. 'Did no one advise you to negotiate? Or meet the leaders privately?' He looked dark and his face held a fury Lilliana had never seen before. He looked almost afraid. 'No. Clearly drama and brute force are your answer, with no thought for the consequences.'

'The souks are outdated,' shouted Lilliana, turning to face Lorcan, but glancing at Brennan. 'We no longer need the minerals, so we no longer need to sell our women. Even you must agree that we need to heal our realm. If our fertility returned, our powers over the Strangers would increase.'

'The people of Daron are rejoicing at the decision,' interrupted Brennan, knowing he was overstepping his rank, but seeing Lilliana's bravado cracking. 'She will be remembered as a leader that put her people first. They see her courage.'

'Really?' raged Lorcan, pacing up to Brennan. Their faces inches apart. 'Do you think they will rejoice when other realms march into Daron and take the women by force? Will they see her courage, as they watch their daughters being slaughtered?'

'Stop it!' screamed Ava. 'This is my fault. I wanted an end to the consort souks. It was the right decision. I put the idea in Lilliana's head.'

'Don't flatter yourself half-Fae,' spat Lilliana, reeling with the realisation that Ava had manipulated her. 'I needed to make my mark. I needed to show the other realms a woman is as good as any man. I am twice as strong as they are, and if standing in the middle of the battle means I get knocked down by both sides, then so be it.'

Lilliana stood tall. She meant every word she shouted, and she would never give Ava the satisfaction of being in charge, even if Lilliana had to take the blame herself. Still, she was surprised to see Lorcan turn abruptly towards Ava.

'And now, war will be inevitable.' Lorcan spoke clearly, but calmly. He stood face to face with Ava, and Ava imagined how close they should be now. They had both lost Foster. He had buried Jess for her, tenderly, with all the kindness you would show someone you cared for, but now he looked detached. Detached, with fear soaking through his expression.

'They won't just come for the women,' he said to Ava, 'They will come for you. And Lilliana.' Lorcan lowered his gaze, and when he spoke next his voice was a whispered rage. 'My body is already used to being beaten, my mind practised at accepting emptiness. But I feel terror when I imagine you being captured.'

'What do you mean?' asked Lilliana, but Lorcan was already half way across the room. He had planned to speak more about Foster, tell them about Carter, and their plans to bring back Jess, but that would have to wait.

'What happened to you Lorcan?' pleaded Lilliana, as Lorcan threw open the heavy gold door and left them.

Ava watched him leave. A shiver ran through her as she thought about their meeting outside the cottage. In reality, she knew very little about Lorcan, but she had seen his scars, she had heard the stories of beatings at the hands of his father. He had been strong, fearless, undefeated. So, she wondered, what had happened to him in these last short months to saturate him with so much dread.

*

The whirlwind of chaos taking place in the Great Hall, allowed Raisa to leave the castle unattended, and unnoticed. She made her way down to the lake, hopeful that the water would restore power to her fading magic. Now, as she twirled droplets around her fingers, she closed her eyes, knowing time was not on her side.

'Raisa.' Heath's voice was loud, but he spoke fondly.

Raisa turned sharply, feeling the familiar voice cut her.

'It has been a long time, Heath,' she replied carefully, deliberately not moving. 'You healed well I see.'

Heath kept his pace steady, without waiting to be invited nearer. When he reached Raisa, he smiled, and pushed the dark hood of her cloak away from her face.

'Not so many years, for us,' he stated. 'Just a mere generation in the Stranger's realm.'

They studied each other, taking in the new lines marking the time they had been apart.

'Why didn't you come back?' Raisa questioned, a sharper edge to her tone.

'I didn't come back, because I had no power. You saw to that. And let's not forget the matter of Kallan.'

'I risked everything to come and find you.' Raisa let her guard down. It made her feel unsafe, but her head was spinning from seeing Heath in front of her. 'If I had been caught crossing over that night, Kallan would have sliced my throat. He was unaware of the Fae living beyond the Oak until the day he died.'

'The day Kallan died,' repeated Heath, raising an eyebrow, his mouth set hard, 'Don't you mean, the day you planned to murder my son?'

Raisa didn't answer. She let Heath search her face. Her eyes a piercing yellow that he had never forgotten; her lips, full and dark red, never quite reaching happiness.

'Did you go back to her?' When Raisa eventually spoke she sounded lost, despite trying to sound as if she didn't care.

'Yes,' Heath didn't hesitate. He had told many lies in his life, but he would never lie about Annie.

'Did you really believe I would come back?' Heath's question was genuine.

'Perhaps,' said Raisa sadly, 'I suppose I wanted you to stop Kallan. Fight for the realm.' She paused, and then tried to add, 'Save me from …'

'From what?' interrupted Heath. 'The man you chose to marry? The man you thought would be picked as leader? You made your choice and you were as guilty as Kallan in plotting to bring me down when it suited you.'

Raisa quickly closed her mouth, startled at the sting in his words.

'Sneaking off to the Stranger's realm and bedding one of them was your downfall Heath,' she spat the words now, moving closer to his face to make her point. He smelt of honeysuckle and Raisa's nerve faltered. She stepped back.

'Make no mistake Raisa,' replied Heath, grabbing her arm tightly and pulling her forward in anger, 'Annie was not a replacement for you. She will burn in my heart forever. I thank the universe for meeting her and there is not a night that goes past when I don't imagine myself entwined with her body. Every night we spent together was worth the world of pain you rained down on me.'

'Enough!' yelled Raisa, 'If that is so, then what could you possibly want here?'

'To help you,' he said plainly.

'What? How can you, help me?'

'You want your position back. I have known you a very long time Raisa. You will not be happy unless you are the leading lady of Daron. And I? I need my children to know me, to be by my side.'

'And you don't want to be leader?' scoffed Raisa.

'Of course I do,' returned Heath. He knew he wouldn't turn the position down. 'I want back, what Kallan took away. And if you help me get it, you will stand by my side, as my equal.'

'Why would you give me that?' Raisa arched an eyebrow over her perfect almond eye. She doubted Heath's intentions were romantic, however hopeful she might silently be.

'Because you saved my life. You took me to Atonia at great risk to yourself. I wish to pay my debt to you.'

Raisa considered his words. She stroked her long fingers down the lapel of his coat and rested them against his chest. He didn't seem to flinch.

'And how will we achieve this?'

'You have an amulet. I remember the day it was given to you. A gift from the Seelie clan, given in thanks for safe passage as they travelled through Daron. Inside is the power to resurrect the dead. It will only work once, and must be used with a powerful incantation.'

'And who do you propose we bring back from the dead?' asked Raisa, becoming animated and concerned.

'Jess. The girl from Blair,' stated Heath. 'She did a great service to the Fae. A Stranger who helps a Fae can be granted new life, in return for her good deed.'

'Where did you hear such nonsense?' Raisa could feel her heart pounding, but she didn't wait for Heath to answer, 'I'm sure Foster and Ava will be very happy,' her mouth twisted as she said their names. The effort not to call them half-Fae was palpable. 'But even if you succeed, how does it help you regain power?'

'Because she is buried in the lake.' Heath looked out across the misty water. He paused as a shimmering turquoise fish burst through the surface to grab a dragonfly. 'This water is unique,' he continued, 'It can carry the force of the ocean, or support the most fragile creature, and when Jess returns she will carry that power. She will be invincible. She will have unimaginable strength within, to conquer this realm and any other.'

Heath smiled now. Weathered, but still handsome he pushed his hands against her hair, and brought them to rest on Raisa's cheeks. She flushed, feeling his intimacy after so long. Her mind raced to absorb the impact of what she'd just heard.

'And I will have a family again,' he finished, 'A family, and power. With Jess on my side no one will cross me.'

Heath moved his mouth to Raisa's ear, 'Which side do you choose to be on this time, Raisa?'

*

'Lorcan. Wait.'

Ava had followed Lorcan, watched him leave the castle and make his way along the side of the lake to where a small path wound like lime velvet towards a hidden embankment packed with small cottages. Each dwelling hovered just above the water, on stilts. In the fractured light it became a charming, homely village.

'Lorcan. I need to talk to you.'

'There is nothing else to say.'

Lorcan spun round as he spoke. His hand swept the air, pushing his voice towards her. Deer, grazing by the water's edge, bounded nervously into the undergrowth.

'Tell me what happened to you?' she asked carefully, closing the space between them.

He didn't speak for a while. She watched as his face silently twisted, reliving fear and pain and then settling on a detached proud stare. Ava felt the air change as owls silently arrived and rested in the trees that shielded the embankment from the meadow. They watched Lorcan with soulful eyes.

'Please,' she pleaded, watching him straighten with pain. His bandages were visible through his shirt.

'Kahors. Do you know it?' he asked, already knowing the answer.

'Yes. Sorcha and I made it to the border about six weeks ago.' It was a rescue that Ava was particularly proud of.

'We had information from Sorcha's neighbour of two young girls that had been taken from Daron. We were told that Kahors was too dangerous a place for us. We were careful.'

'But your rescue was successful.' Lorcan looked almost impressed, Ava thought, and then she decided she must be mistaken.

'Yes. How do you know that?' Ava waited, but no response came, 'There is a network growing within the realms. Of course they have to keep secrets and not be discovered, but messages were relayed to the girls, and they met us just inside the border on market day. We hid them and smuggled them out in darkness.'

Lorcan winced. Ava stepped the final yards separating them and grabbed at Lorcan's shirt with no warning.

'Show me' she demanded, not waiting for an answer, ripping up his shirt, and moving the bandages down.

'The Lords of Kahors may not have fertility,' said Lorcan, as Ava stared wide eyed at the three bloody lacerations running across his stomach, 'But they have a supply of poisonous magic that is ruthless against their own kind. I do not possess the knowledge to heal this quickly. It will linger for a while yet, as a reminder of their anger, and my lack of control over my subjects.'

'What?' Ava jolted and searched Lorcan's eyes. 'You mean me? And Sorcha?'

Lorcan nodded, and the edges of his mouth lifted in a smile.

'I was looking for Foster,' he said, shivering at the touch of her hand as she replaced the cloth covering the wounds, 'I had information he was staying near the fountains of Kahors. I was recognised and taken. But, it is possible I trusted the wrong people.'

Ava's throat stung as she fought the urge to cry. 'You were punished for what I did,' she said, struggling to get the words out.

'Yes,' replied Lorcan simply. 'But rather that, than your capture.' He paused, and when he spoke again his words were calm and even, like a story he had dreaded telling.

'They kept me chained for weeks, but I lost track of time. I thought it was months. There was no night or day. No light to feel safe by. I was alone. They came in every so often to tell me that day, would be the day I died. That I would die alone, and no one would mourn me, because no one would know I was dead or what had happened to me. I would be placed in a pit in the ground. And people would walk on me and not know I was there. Someone would come and add poison to the wounds, reopening them and stretching them until they wouldn't stop bleeding. I started to look forward to death, to think of ways to rip the wounds open further and let death in.'

When Lorcan finished speaking he focused back on Ava.

'I could not bear this to happen to you,' he said, flinching at the shock frozen on her face, and the angry way she knotted her skirts through her hands.

'Is there more?' she sobbed, almost unable to get the words from her chest. 'More wounds like this?'

'No,' he lied, not wanting to upset her more.

'How did you get away?' Ava wiped at her face, sniffing loudly, and trying to calm the jolting sobs grabbing at her chest.

'The man I told you I met. He was a guard. A guard with contacts. I owe him my life.'

'You mean Carter?' questioned Ava suspiciously.

'Yes,' Lorcan wondered at Ava's sudden change of tone. 'Foster had taken lodging with him in the centre of Kahors, where the fountains merge, forming a giant monument to water. Carter has gathered knowledge of sorcery from many realms.'

'And you don't think it's unusual, or odd, that this Fae takes Foster in, and then agrees to free you, and now, all of a sudden wants to offer more help?'

Ava was about to launch into the story of meeting Carter at the castle. It must be the same Fae, she decided, it was too much of a coincidence. She sensed Brennan was already suspicious. But a man's voice shouting her name cut across her thoughts, sending new tears spilling down her cheeks.

'Foster!'

She yelled in loud sobs, throwing her arms around his neck and causing the bewildered flurry of owls to scatter across the sky.

*

Raisa was crossing the courtyard when she saw Carter chatting with Brennan's guards near the entrance to the kitchens.

'Hello again. It's Carter isn't it? May I speak with you, alone.' She pulled her self up straight and glared down her nose at the guards, reminding them that she used to be in charge. They quickly made their excuses.

As soon as the others had left, Raisa turned on Carter, her voice tight and controlled.

'What do you think you're doing? Why have you brought Heath in on this? He's just told me your whole plan. Except,' she hissed, 'He seems to think he will be in charge?'

Carter took a deep breath, but his face was brash, confident. 'Is this really the place to discuss this? If we are spotted together, Lilliana will be told.' He ran a finger down Raisa's sharp cheekbone, 'We can't have your little girl finding out your terrible plan for revenge can we?' His voice was arrogant.

'Just answer my question,' sneered Raisa, pulling roughly at Carter's finger, smacking it away from her face.

'I'm just covering all the bases,' he stated, leaning against a wall and casually checking who could be listening. 'He was asking questions around Kahors. I got word he planned to come back to Daron. The last thing we need is your ex-leader poking about here.'

'So you thought you'd work with him too? How am I supposed to trust you Carter?'

'I'm not working with him.' Carter didn't look at all fazed by the fierce yellow blazing from Raisa's eyes. 'I'm keeping him close.' He took one more quick glance around. 'Look, he's damaged, he's tired, he just wants Foster and Ava to know him again. We don't need him, but at least we get to raise this girl from the lake with no fuss. And when that's done, when the time is right, I'll slice his heart out. You people need to learn to relax. Not every problem needs brute force.'

A smile played at the edges of Raisa's mouth. She was starting to like the idea of Heath being around, even if only a short time. And, a thought was fizzing quietly at the back of her mind. She planned a future where Jess was under her control, her weapon, and she was in charge of Daron, but now she added Heath to that future. She wouldn't tell Carter, he didn't need to know. She was tired of men using her and, finally, she would beat them at their own game.

*

Carter stood on the village green in Blair. The early morning sun warmed the Stranger's world. He thought about his meeting with Raisa last night while he watched Maria getting her café ready for the new day. Carter knew she was Fae, even if the Strangers blindly going about their business didn't. But then he'd always known. He'd known from the day she'd found him, all those years ago. A child, shivering by the arch in the clearing. A Fae child abandoned on the wrong side for Daron. He watched her elegant movements as she lifted cloths and let them fall gently to the tables. She could have used magic, he smiled, but she never did. She tried to fit in. Carter's brows furrowed as he thought about the times, growing up, when Maria had begged him to fit in, to accept he would never know who his parents were. To move beyond it. He could never fault her love for him, but he knew he had broken her heart when he left.

'Why you watching her so intently?' The voice startled him, but he had been expecting company. 'Not one of them is she? Want us to slice a dagger across her throat?'

'No,' hissed Carter. He turned to face the man talking, and noticed he wore the collar of a priest. The Order really is gathering momentum, he mused. 'The delivery must be important, if they're not trusting it to a foot soldier,' he stated out loud.

'Yes,' replied the man, looking perplexed, 'This weapon is critical. Nothing can get in the way. Are you sure that woman is not a threat? I've watched you stare at her for half an hour.'

Carter grabbed the man's throat. 'I said,' he growled, 'Leave her out of this.'

'OK, OK.' The priest rubbed at his throat as Carter released him, 'Just make sure the delivery arrives on time. You made a deal, and like I said, nothing can be allowed to get in the way.'

The man walked away, shrugging his coat closer around his body. Maria looked up briefly, alerted by the movement. Carter pulled his hat down over his ears, and pushed his face inside his jacket.

With the priest out of earshot, Carter smiled to himself and spoke under his breath, 'Don't worry. Nothing will get in the way.' He almost wanted someone to hear. 'You are all so alike. Fae and Strangers, arrogant and naïve. You both seek to own each other, and destroy what you cannot have. Jess will return, and she will be a weapon. But, none of you will be able to control her and I will watch as mayhem and carnage unfurl. I will watch the realms fall as Strangers and Fae beg for mercy. I will have revenge on you all. I will watch you die, one by one, and you won't even remember my name.'

Chapter 5

The day continued to heat itself towards a blistering noon in Blair, causing Brennan to remove his jacket as he walked towards Cedric's garden. He had ventured over to the Stranger's side several times since he'd discovered his father was alive and each trip stirred a mixture of comfort and loss.

Cedric felt Brennan's presence long before he saw him approach. He had waited patiently for his son to walk up to the gate, and now stood scowling at the marked arms of the lean soldier.

'Would you have those scars if I had not abandoned you?'

'Old man,' replied Brennan softly, 'It has been a long time since I cried over the pieces of yesterday. Without the ties of family, I found my own way. Do not worry for me, each of these scars is a sign that I continue to survive.'

'Still, they will serve as a reminder to me each time I see you, of the pain I have caused.'

Brennan said nothing. He was starting to understand that Cedric needed torment like fuel.

'One day, soon, I will tell you why I left. Tell you of the horror I caused. Your life was better with me gone.'

Brennan heard Cedric speak, but didn't make eye contact with him. He wasn't sure he needed to know more. It would make him start to care and that, was a distraction. He toyed with the petals of a honeysuckle flower, wondering what to say.

Finally, he settled on the subject that was bothering him most.

'Do you know of a Fae called Carter?' he asked casually. And when Cedric's face looked blank, Brennan told him everything he knew about the man he didn't trust.

'If your instinct says all is not well, you should listen.' Cedric felt pride as he spoke, and then inwardly told himself that was not his right. 'I will ask around, and keep an ear to the whispering of the breeze,' he added, 'But, it is possible this Fae is just a chancer. There will be many more now young Lilliana is in charge.'

Brennan smiled slightly.

'And how is she? I imagine she is not easy to protect?' Cedric had noticed the smile.

'Easy?' huffed Brennan. 'She is stubborn. She is opinionated. She is defiant.'

Cedric smiled. 'Are those not traits you admire?' he asked, already knowing the answer his son would give.

Brennan smiled again, and looked at Cedric. He caught the old man trying to make his face serious.

'Yes,' stated Brennan, and then he turned his face away, so Cedric couldn't read him. 'I admire her very much.'

*

It was only later, long after Brennan had returned to Daron, that Cedric finally picked apart the knot of time that had bothered him all afternoon. He didn't remember the name, Carter, or the man that Brennan described. But there had been a boy once. Abandoned, with no hope of ever knowing who left him. But he was half-Fae. Maria had asked Cedric to confirm it, but Cedric had known by then that Maria would keep him. He was shy at first, but inquisitive. Maria taught him to be independent and strong. And then, he had left her. The inevitable, warped, irony of a parents duty. Maria hadn't spoken of him for years. Cedric sensed she didn't know what had become of him. Could they be the same man? Cedric muttered to himself, trying to force a picture of Maria's boy in his mind. His hair was blonde. Unusual for a Fae. His name was Carraeir. Yes, that had been his name. Carraeir.

*

'Do you think Lorcan is right?' Lilliana turned away from Brennan as she spoke. She wanted to see if he would move closer to her on the balcony, and she was annoyed that he'd not been in the castle earlier when she wanted him. 'Do you believe war is inevitable?'

From here, she could see out beyond the lake. The evening air was warm and only the slightest shiver rippled up her spine as she sensed Brennan behind her.

'The rumours, through the villages, speak of a battle coming,' replied Brennan, watching Lilliana's shoulders pull back as the gap between them closed.

Both stood and watched the curly hazel trees, planted to one side of the lake, come to life with light. The Fae, decorating the branches with streams of coloured glass, were like busy ants under the guidance of the moon.

'They prepare for Varatic,' said Brennan, more to himself. 'A celebration of the sun, and how it has warmed the Fae, since our time began. Many choose to honour the life they have here. It is enough for them, to live in peace.'

'And tonight,' answered Lilliana, 'They smile at the moon and let it fill their souls.'

Brennan glanced over, surprised Lilliana would remember the words of the Elders, and saw she was smiling. It was rare, and he moved to her side, turning his head to stare. She fought the desire to stare back.

'Your people do not want war,' he said quietly, still looking at her. 'And, I am afraid that Lorcan speaks the truth, when he says there is a price on your head.'

Lilliana turned her head slowly, met his gaze directly, but her expression was soft, probably the most vulnerable he had ever seen her. 'I will not bend, or break to anyone's will. I will hold on to what I believe, whatever the price.'

'I know,' he replied quietly.

'Are you with me Brennan? Whatever the price? Are you with me?' Her eyes questioned his, and for a brief, mad moment Brennan wanted to hold her.

'Yes. Always,' was all he said.

Something shifted between them in those precious seconds. For the shortest time, Brennan moved beyond protector, beyond friendship. Neither knew where they stood. Lilliana fought with the thumping in her chest. There was no air between them. Nothing existed beyond the balcony. As one faltering breath followed another, the cry of the wolves sliced the evening and jolted them back to the roles they felt destined to play.

'What do you want though, Lady Lilliana?' Brennan didn't move, but his voice resumed that of a soldier. 'What will you do next?'

Lilliana straightened her back and considered her answer. She could not be, would not be, sidetracked.

'What I want,' she replied, looking out towards the lake, 'Is what I've always wanted. To be leader. To be dominant over the Strangers.' She sighed, wanting to savour the sweetness of their moment, before it was lost. 'Let the realms fight me, and let them fight one another. Let my people see who they can turn to. I will deliver us to strength and fertility. To greatness.'

'You should consider this' cautioned Brennan, 'To encourage chaos to gain the support of your people is dangerous.' His brows furrowed in concern. He almost reached out and touched her, desperate to make her re-consider.

Lilliana closed her eyes and inhaled the scent of evening primrose, curling from the brickwork. She wanted him to move closer, but she knew the moment was gone.

'Thank you Brennan,' she said curtly, when his touch didn't come. She picked up the long skirt of her feathered gown and turned away sharply, to dismiss him. 'That will be all, for tonight.'

*

Ava knew, as she stepped through the old stone arch, that wolves would be waiting by the Oak in Daron. They had been there every time she'd passed through in the last few months. As if they had instructions, from Lorcan, to watch for her. Now, as she approached the chocolate brown female, she put out her hand. She'd been making progress with this one. Ava met the palest yellow, inquisitive gaze. The wolf's head was hard, but like velvet, as it bumped Ava's out stretched hand and nestled there.

'I've stayed away for three days, little lady.' Ava's mouth curved to a smile as the wolf sat, resting against her legs. 'Now you tell your master, I need to see him. I need his help.' As she spoke absently to the attentive creature, she thought about Toni's request, '*I need flowers from the Forest of the Sith. Some of the local children are unwell. If Lorcan will allow you to pick them, I could heal so many people, so easily. I need the hornbeam and the cherry plum. I do not expect this to be an easy task.*'

The wolf bent her head back and observed Ava. As it's tongue lolled to one side, Ava wondered if she was being laughed at. 'Yes, I will ask nicely. And, may his Lordship not be too smug, when he finds out I need him,' she whispered down, bending to almost meet the wolf's face.

The other wolves circled closer and came to sit around Ava, but she wasn't afraid. One by one, they lifted their heads to the purple dusk and howled together. It was a haunting sound, that made Ava close her eyes and inhale the early evening. She felt the air change against her skin and let the familiar heat climb over her body as she waited.

'Am I expected to knock this time too?' His voice was clear and close, even though Ava hadn't heard his arrival. She wondered how long she had waited, it seemed only a minute, but the light had now faded considerably, leaving a navy mist to float across the meadow towards the lake.

'Your sarcasm is hilarious,' she mused, trying to ignore how his fingers brushed her leg as he pulled playfully at the wolf's ear.

Lorcan looked quizzically at Ava, making her burn. 'I only meant, that you have requested to see me. So I assume you were expecting my arrival?' He continued to watch her and Ava felt the inky stare suffocate her.

'I know you told me to stay in Blair, in the cottage, but I … well I just want to know what's happening. And how Foster is?' Ava decided to start her request gently. She glanced down towards his stomach to see if any bandages were visible, wondering how his wounds were.

Lorcan continued to stare. 'I have long since learnt that you will not bend to my will,' he said calmly, 'And I am surprised that you stayed away for, let me see, nearly three days.' Ava was sure he was laughing at her behind the scowl. 'But if you have come here to tell me that Foster and I cannot bring back Jess, you are too late. Preparations have already started and the amulet will be broken tomorrow.'

'Have you totally lost the plot?' Ava raged, forgetting she had come to talk about collecting herbs for Toni. 'We talked about this, with Foster. I thought we agreed to at least wait until we know what the other realms plan next.' Ava's eyes pleaded at Lorcan even though her voice was tight and full of spite. He could feel the heat of her breath as she ranted.

'No,' Lorcan replied, holding her stare. 'You told us what you thought we should do. We listened. But we didn't change our mind.' He held his face close to her, daring her to argue back.

Ava was exasperated. Lorcan stood there, with all the arrogance of the man she had met months earlier. Nothing had changed. She felt a sensation of falling, of being plunged into a deep well with no means to climb out.

'I wish Jess had never met you.' The words surged from Ava. Words, that should have been true, but she knew she didn't mean them, 'I wish, I had never met you.'

She watched Lorcan flinch. The tiniest movement, that showed her she had made a cut. 'Does she mean nothing to you? Do I mean nothing to you?' She intended her words to make the wound deeper.

His hands moved up, violently, and his grip around her arms made Ava gasp with shock.

'Let go of me,' she hissed. 'There is something cold inside you Lorcan. And sometimes, I don't think you care that it's there.'

Lorcan's grip faltered, but he didn't let go completely. Ava could feel his fingers still burning against her skin. As if he had somehow transferred some of his pain to her. She stayed still, letting his body lean against her slightly. When he raised his head, Ava could see herself in his inky eyes. The line deepening between his brows kept her quiet.

'You mistake me Ava, and that is a pity. I am no longer your enemy.'

'I hate your riddles. I've always hated your riddles.' Ava jutted her chin towards Lorcan, daring him to challenge her.

'You want to know why I trust Carter?' Lorcan's voice was harsh and low. 'You want to know why I would take part in such dreadful sorcery?'

'Yes,' she raged, 'I really do want to know, because there is no excuse.' Her eyes were fierce and Lorcan felt the warmth of her breath as she threw the words out.

'Because we all control so little.' His voice faded slightly as he replied, but Ava knew he meant every word. She felt his fingers burn her arm again. 'Because there was a time, when I thought I would rule this land, and I believed the Strangers were all bad. My days were simple, and even the beatings at the hands of my father had reason and logic. If not for Foster, I would still be that ridiculous fool. He is my brother, and from the day he came to my realm, he has been saving me. I owe him. Everything. And there is nothing I wouldn't do to keep him from ruin.'

Ava's head jolted up. She studied Lorcan. 'Keep him from ruin?' she questioned.

'You think he has not had time to think about his past? To wonder why he was even born in the first place? Did his father love him, or was he always made to be the sacrifice? He has no loyalty any longer to your lands or mine. In his eyes he fits nowhere. The only person that made him feel strong, invincible, was Jess.'

A sickening terror was building in Ava's stomach and crawling up her chest. She had never considered any of this. She had blindly assumed Foster would just go on being, Foster. 'This is his idea?' she asked weakly, 'All, his idea?'

'Yes. He wants Jess more than he wants life itself. And if he can't have Jess, well ...'

Ava's knees buckled slightly as Lorcan fought with what to say next.

'There is nothing I wouldn't do,' he repeated, 'I cannot lose

Foster.'

Chapter 6

The sun rose on a new day in Daron. Misty, sultry, and full of hope. As it moved higher against the mountains, the Fae from the villages gathered under the curly hazel trees to celebrate Varatic.

'I plan to join them,' Lorcan said to Lilliana, as they watched from a castle balcony. 'A celebration of the sun reminds us all of our place. And, that perhaps we can still hope for peace, together.' Lorcan paused. 'Our father never set foot in the villages.' And then he asked, 'Will you join me sister?' He wondered what her answer would be. Wondered what she would say if she saw Foster there.

'Do you plan to go?' Lilliana looked to Brennan for the

answer.

'Yes,' he replied, smiling. 'When I was a boy, my father, Cedric, would let me drink a toast of health to the villagers. I can still remember my first sip of scorpion wine.' He held out his arm to Lilliana, fixing her with green eyes, 'I would be happy to escort you, My Lady.'

*

Carter could barely see the hazel trees from the far edge of the lake. He looked at the amulet in his hand, let his fingers toy with the silver clasp. He wondered if even the Seelie clan had known the power it contained, when they had given it as a gift to Raisa. The power to resurrect the dead. How was that safe in anyone's hands? he wondered. A smile spread across his face, and he wanted to laugh out loud at the stupidity of everyone around him. He was about to unscrew the clasp, when a group of soldiers caught his eye. Tucking the amulet in a pocket, Carter sat on the edge of the water, pretending to fill a bottle. He watched with growing intrigue and unrest as four of Brennan's men marched across the meadow carrying a bloodied bundle.

*

'Take Lilli back to the castle.' Lorcan roared his command at Brennan as he watched the soldiers walking towards them.

'Those are my men. My responsibility,' argued Brennan. 'One of them is injured.'

'Did you not hear me?' replied Lorcan, turning to stare at Brennan, the sick feeling in his stomach reeling over and over. He could tell the body was female; from the fabric covering the legs of the body; from the hand bobbing against the soldier's thigh. Every nerve in his body told him it was Ava.

'I answer to Lilliana,' stated Brennan defiantly, and he looked towards the woman standing silently beside him. She looked young, and weary.

'I stay, with my brother.' The words were uttered with quiet confusion.

Lorcan had no energy to argue back. He watched every step the soldiers took, wondering why they walked so slowly, but wishing they would never reach him. As the blood soaked through the sheeting covering their cargo, Lorcan sank to his knees, knowing that the body they carried was dead. He could hear no heartbeat, feel no warmth. He knew the price on Ava's head was high, but he'd thought they had more time.

'Ava?' His lips hardly moved as he muttered her name. If he opened his mouth to say it any louder, he knew for certain he would be sick.

'My Lord,' said the first solider solemnly, placing the bundle on the ground near Lorcan. 'We found her at the edge of the realm. She was already dead. Her wounds were deep.'

The soldiers stepped away from the body, nodded to Lorcan and Lilliana, then looked to Brennan waiting to be dismissed. Lorcan would remember afterwards, the creak of the soldier's boots as they walked away, the slow breathy noise Brennan made when he replied to his men. He would remember his sister kneeling down beside him, pausing to squirm, but then not caring that her dress was pressing into blood. The finely tuned distractions that kept him from raising his head towards the mountains, and screaming.

Chapter 7

You were warned in Kahors.
Your subjects did not heed the warning.
So, we have taken away their hope.
May you bleed, and never heal.

Lilliana read the words out loud. The note, so full of hate, was crafted from large curly letters on brown parchment. She had pulled it from the top of a bloodied boot.

'Let me take her.' Brennan placed his hand slowly on Lorcan's shoulder as he spoke, 'I will take her to the palace.'

Lorcan remained silent. Brennan's voice rang around him like an echo. He touched the bandages around his ribs. The wounds that never heal.

'No,' said Lilliana, 'We should leave them.' She pressed her hand lightly against the cloth, covering the body. Her heart ached for her brother, although she knew she would have to pretend to care that Ava was dead. Still, she mused, she had been gutsy, a fool maybe, but definitely brave – for a Half Fae.

As Lilliana stood to leave, she took Brennan's hand from Lorcan's shoulder and held it in her own. Brennan shivered from the intimacy. He had never felt her fingers hold him before. 'We are leaving,' she said resolutely, but Brennan saw a warmth in her eyes that made her face glow.

A woman running towards them caught Brennan's line of sight, but he was reluctant to move his gaze from Lilliana.

'Oh God. What's happened? Who is that?' The voice was loud, growing in pitch with every word.

Brennan rushed towards the figure, dropping Lilliana's hand, leaving her standing alone.

He shouted her name as he embraced her.

'Ava.'

*

Toni shook her head at Cedric as she walked up to the open front door. 'There is a sickness spreading amongst the children. I have never seen it here before. The only medicine that makes them well is the one I press from flowers from the Forest of the Sith.'

'But you are concerned?' said Cedric, noticing the weary, troubled look on Toni's face 'You have been helping the sick for many years. Why is this so different Atonia? Are you concerned your magic will alert The Order to our presence?'

Toni sighed, heavily. 'If only that was my biggest problem,' she said, rubbing at her temples.

Cedric took her hands and smiled gently. 'The flowers, the cherry plum and hornbeam, can Ava find them anywhere other than the Forest of the Sith? I'm sure we do not need to be concerned.'

Toni shook her head, 'No. The ones I need are watered by the Asrai and infused with power.'

'It's strange,' mused Cedric, determined to chip away at Toni's reluctance to speak her mind, 'I didn't even realise you kept such flowers. I didn't know they had such medicinal qualities.'

'That's just it,' replied Toni, searching the old man's face, but not knowing where to find the answer, 'I had forgotten

I had them. They have been in bottles, unused for two generations. The people here had no illnesses that needed such treatments.'

Cedric held her hands tightly, unused to seeing Toni less than calm. The line between her brows deepened.

'So how can it be?' she finished, 'That now, in one short month, there is not one flower left. Not one petal. All gone. I have used every last one.'

*

'We thought you dead,' Lilliana spoke coldly.

She had moved to join Brennan's side, still reeling from the absolute way he had left her hand in mid air. Lorcan had not moved. He remained slumped over the body on the grass, his head lower than before.

'Who is it?' asked Ava slowly. In just a few short months she had seen so much blood and death around her, but in truth, the sight would always make her head spin and her stomach crawl inside itself. The thought of getting used to death, terrified her.

Lorcan still didn't speak. He didn't lift his head to look at any of them. His shoulders felt knotted as he fought to take a deep breath. Slowly he peeled the cloth, already crusted with blood, away from the bundle.

Ava watched in horror, as the body was slowly revealed. Deep cuts covered the arms and legs, intricate carvings of swirls and dots. Gouged out to mark, in blood and flesh, the Fae symbols of majesty. The symbols of water and power. They smothered the stomach and chest, making Ava wonder if they had been made after death. And finally, she looked at the face. She had known long before though. She had known when she saw the boots, but hope had lingered. Now she sank to her knees, opposite the silent Lorcan.

Sorcha.

Beautiful, fearless, Sorcha.

Scarred and broken.

Determined and ambitious.

Dead.

'This is your doing,' yelled Lilliana surging towards Ava, 'You brought this down on all of us. They are taunting us. Who knows what is coming next. You and...,' she pointed at Sorcha's torn body, 'This ridiculous crusader. Thinking you are some kind of saviours.'

Ava shook her head, her eyes wide with horror. She wasn't a saviour. That wasn't what she was doing.

'Lilli. Stop,' urged Brennan, grabbing Lilliana's arm and pulling her back. She didn't pull her arm away. She liked the feeling of him holding her. In another time or place, she might have turned and pressed against him to shut the anger out. 'There is plenty to say, but this is not the right time.' Brennan was still speaking to Lilliana, but he was looking anxiously at Lorcan, who was bent over Sorcha's body, tracing his fingers against the marks running down her cheek. Her body scarred forever by the symbols they valued. Brennan watched as Lorcan's shoulders collapsed with emotion. He could feel a wave of darkness sweep across each of them.

'I will take you back now My Lady,' he stated formally, starting to move Lilliana away from the scene. 'You need to be under protection.'

Minutes passed in silence. It felt like hours. Ava stayed on her knees, not caring that her gulped sobs were filling the space between her and Lorcan. She wanted to reach out to Sorcha, find a connection, but she felt like the intruder. Lorcan said nothing. He didn't raise his head. Through her swelling eyes, she saw his shoulders tremble every minute or so. She wondered if he was crying. She pondered touching his arm, but the silence was growing thicker and edged with menace.

Finally, in desperation for comfort, Ava spoke. 'Say something, please, Lorcan?' Her words were hard to distinguish, her mouth was twisted in distress, staring at Sorcha.

Lorcan's body slumped at the sound of her voice. Ava saw him struggle to inhale. As if he wanted to speak, but the words were lost, or just impossible to say. Finally, he gently covered Sorcha's body, and scooped her into his arms, standing in one graceful movement.

'Where are you taking her?' asked Ava, through more gulps.

Lorcan ignored her question, but slowly raised his head and fixed her with a glare that froze her heart.

His mouth trembled, balanced on the edge of madness. When he finally spoke, his voice was raw, 'I thought, this was you.'

He looked wounded, exposed. And before Ava had the chance to exhale, he was gone.

*

Heath walked slowly up behind Carter. Both stood and watched the scene unfolding on the other side of the lake. Carter sensed the forest animals, drinking from the lake, were spying on him, and he glared at them disrespectfully.

'What would you have done, if Ava had been delivered back, bloody and sliced?'

Carter knew Heath was there, he spoke calmly to show he was not intimidated.

'I would have slowly gouged your eyes out and sent them to your mother.' Heath moved his mouth close to Carter's ear as he spoke, hissing the words. There was no trace of humour in the response.

'Wait.' Carter snapped his head round. 'You think this was me?'

'Do not think for one second I have not been watching you. You are more than capable of this.'

Carter laughed. A deep, throaty laugh of enjoyment. 'I wish I had thought of it,' he remarked lightly. 'It's genius. The palace will be in chaos. Wondering when the next attack will be.' Carter was smiling. 'But, sadly, I cannot take the credit.'

Heath's mouth tightened slightly at the glibness of Carter.

'If any harm comes to Ava, at your hand or another's, your tongue will not be so slippery.'

'Heath,' cajoled Carter, touching the older man's arm, 'Tonight we will have Jess back. The palace will be too busy to notice. You will unite your family. This realm is yours.'

Carter smiled and started to walk away. 'Besides,' he called back, 'If you did decide to gouge out my eyes, I do not have a mother for you to send them to.' He chuckled as he walked away.

'Really?' said Heath loudly, turning to watch the smile fall from Carter's face. 'I already told you, I have been watching you. Do not underestimate me Carter. You and I both know Maria would be saddened to see the man you have become.'

*

Foster knew it was risky to wait in Lilliana's room for her, but it seemed strange not to see her before he joined Carter at the lake. Perhaps, because he knew she would not approve of his plan to bring Jess back, better to show her he was alive now, than when she no longer wanted to speak to him. He knew, in his heart, this was a bad idea, but the longer he waited, the harder it was to walk away and not see her annoying face. He smiled, remembering the chasing and fighting when she was younger. She had adored him, he mused, right to the end. She had gone against Kallan, for him. He owed her at least his thanks. Just in case he never saw her again.

'Is it really you?' Lilliana forced back tears as she put her arms around Foster.

'You look different,' he laughed, pulling back to look at her. 'Where has Lorcan's bratty little sister gone?' Then he smiled gently, 'You look beautiful Lilli,' he said, and he meant it. 'Being leader suits you.'

'You may be alone in your opinion,' she said, wondering

why the words she had waited so long to hear, didn't flood her with happiness. She studied Foster's face, noting he looked more serious and slightly defeated. 'They want to marry me off,' she added solemnly.

'Now, that would be worth seeing.' Foster's eyes sparkled, 'I can just see you kicking and screaming your way through these corridors,' he laughed.

'Of course,' Lilliana looked at Foster from under huge eyelashes. 'You are the rightful heir to all this. Heath was your father. Our family stole this from you.' She waited to see what Foster would say. For so many years, the idea of ruling with Foster had always been her perfect ending.

Foster took her hands in his. 'Lilli, I don't want this.' He looked around as he spoke, amused that he really didn't care for this magnificent place, and knowing everything he wanted was at the bottom of the lake. 'You will grow to be a fine leader, I know it. And you will find a man worthy of your unique ability - to annoy and aggravate.' He was smiling now, and as Lilliana lost hope that Foster would ever be hers, she realised that she didn't mind. It didn't hurt.

'Which one are you?' she asked, changing the subject, but not letting go of his hands. 'Fae, or Stranger? Do you feel like one of them? What is it like?'

Foster laughed out loud. 'I will not choose one, or the other. I'm just me. Still me,' he replied, admiring her honesty in asking. 'And you must work to get along with Ava. She is my sister, and she is a good person.'

'Aw,' she said, screwing up her face, reminding Foster of the petulant child she used to be. 'It will never work. She is no Fae. She is nothing like you.'

'She is everything like me,' chastised Foster. 'You should try to make her welcome.'

'I shall not,' stated Lilliana, raising her eyebrows and pursing her lips.

Foster rested his chin against the top of Lilliana's head and she closed her eyes trying to capture the moment.

'If you do not make my sister welcome, I will pull your ringlets and put frogs under your covers.' There was laughter in Foster's voice, but Lilliana detected the absence of joy that used to edge his words.

She moved her head, so she could look at Foster's face again. 'Do your worst, Foster,' she said, wanting to sound light, but feeling the burn of tears in her throat. 'I can defend myself against a frog.'

'Will I always be welcome in your realm, My Lady Lilliana?' he asked quietly, seriously.

'Yes, Foster,' she whispered, not opening her eyes, 'You, of all the people in all the realms, will be the most welcome.'

Foster gently kissed the back of Lilliana's hand, and bowed his head. He smiled, knowing she would see the humour in his actions, as well as the sincerity.

Lilliana stood, staring out from her balcony, long after Foster had left. If she had pulled herself from the images of childhood racing around her mind, she would have noticed Brennan trying to leave without being noticed. She might have asked him, how much he had heard or seen. If she hadn't been so lost in the memories of Foster, and the life she was leaving behind, she might have noticed the way Brennan watched her holding Foster's hands. She might have wondered at the sadness in Brennan's eyes, as he listened to the easy way Foster teased her. She might have seen him walk away, having felt their history fill the room, in a way he knew he could never achieve.

Chapter 8

The night was purple, deep and velvety as Foster joined Lorcan and Carter by the lake. Remnants of Varatic hung motionless from trees fringing the side of the water. The stillness was conspicuous and deafening. Not a single creature foraged or swam.

'I thought perhaps you'd changed your mind?' said Carter, taking the amulet from his pocket. 'Would you rather delay another day? After the death I mean. So traumatic for you all I'm sure?' Carter kept his voice low and calm. He didn't want to delay another second, but he was used to playing the long game.

'Perhaps we should wait,' added Lorcan. He would do

anything for Foster, to keep him from harming himself, but the threat from the other realms; to Ava and his sister, was consuming him. 'Wait until we know we are bringing Jess back to somewhere safe.'

'No,' stormed Foster. 'You know why I'm here. The only reason I came back. For Jess. Your fight is not my fight Lorcan.' He turned his head to look directly at his oldest friend, 'Not any more. When this is over, and Jess is with me, we will leave this place.'

'What?' exclaimed Lorcan, 'But this is your home.'

Foster was about to reply. About to tell Lorcan that his mind was made up. He would show no favour to the Fae, or the Strangers. He had tasted the bliss of being with Jess, and that was all he needed. But someone else had been listening. Tucked away in the secrecy of darkness, someone listened who wanted him to stay in Daron, perhaps even more than Lorcan did.

Heath rushed towards his son, wanting to close the gap of time, 'Foster. Please stay. Let me know you. Let me be your father.'

'What did you say? Who are you?' hissed Lorcan, pulling a blade from this coat and stepping in the space between Heath and Foster.

Foster reeled back at the sight of his father lurching from no where.

Carter exhaled loudly and squinted, visibly annoyed that no

one was sticking to his plan. He would not watch this unravel.

'Heath?' breathed Foster, his eyes wide and his jaw refusing to close, 'You're not dead? All this time, and you're not dead?'

'Can we leave the reunions until later? We need the girl now,' stated Carter, annoyance spilling from every word.

Foster continued to stare at his father, a nausea of confusion growing in his stomach.

'What?' asked Lorcan sharply, turning abruptly to Carter. 'Why do you need Jess right now?' He wondered at how displeased Carter was suddenly looking. 'Why do *you* need her at all?'

Foster ignored everyone, except Heath. 'Why now? What is it you want that you came back now? What about the times I needed a father? Who was supposed to show me how to become a man?' Foster could feel the anger mixing in his stomach, rising up through his words. 'You didn't even show when I was about to be murdered by Kallan.'

'Enough of this,' shouted Carter, holding the amulet up to the moon and speaking ancient words that made the inked marks on Lorcan's shoulder burn like nettles.

'Did you make me on purpose?' continued Foster. 'Did you know all along, I would be taken and raised as a sacrifice?'

Carter's words spiralled towards the amulet, delving inside, turning it's contents into a haze of diamond mist that coiled and circled above the lake.

'No.' Heath shot back quickly, raising his hand to reach out to Foster. 'I loved Annie with every breathe I took. I possessed everything it is possible to desire, but I gave it up in a heartbeat to love her.'

Lorcan tried to block the other voices out. He concentrated on the pain iced across the symbols on his body. Slowly, but with sickening clarity he started to translate some of Carter's words.

Weapon

Power

Rise

'Foster' he shouted, catching the look of triumph starting to crawl across Carter's face, 'Something is not right. We need to end this.'

'No. Don't listen to him Foster,' retaliated Heath, 'We can get Jess back. She will be stronger, better. We can be a family again.'

'What do you mean? Stronger?' shot Lorcan, feeling more words from Carter's continued whispers.

Chaos

Slaughter

'I don't want to be a family with you.' Foster's voice was icy, detached. 'I just want to be with Jess.' He felt the ache of Heath's words ...*I possessed everything it is possible to desire, but I gave it up in a heartbeat to love her ...* 'Whatever it takes,' he finished, in a whisper.

The mist started to spin, faster and faster, growing until it was a glittering cone hovering just above the waters surface.

'We have to stop,' yelled Lorcan.

'Oh, it is too late for that my friend,' replied Carter, breaking from the trance of words and smiling. 'The new, improved Jess is on her way, and she will be the greatest weapon you have ever seen.'

'This won't be Jess,' screamed Lorcan to Foster. 'I want you to have her back, believe me. But what kind of hell will you have condemned her too?'

Carter walked towards Foster, smiling as if they were brothers. 'The time for talking is over, look how the magic descends down through the water.'

Everyone turned and watched the water open, accepting the coil of mist, as if solid.

'All you have to do, is collect her. Whoever carried her in, must carry her out.' Carter's voice was calm, measured. It was nearly over. He was so close.

'We can do this together, son,' said Heath slowly, 'You'll be reunited with your love, and we can rule together. That's your destiny.'

Foster ignored Heath and faced Lorcan.

'No,' pleaded Lorcan, 'It won't be the Jess you had before. She … It will be something different. What if her soul is gone?'

'You carried her in Lorcan,' stated Foster, surprising Carter and Heath. 'You did that for me. You buried her with honour and respect.'

'Yes.' Lorcan didn't think he could bear the weight on his chest any longer. He had known Foster long enough to know every expression on his face. They had suffered together, laughed together. He knew the impossible choice he was heading towards.

'Then you will carry her back for me,' Foster lifted his chin, and looked braver than Lorcan had ever seen him. 'Her soul is strong. She will not bend to the will of others. I will take her far away from here.'

'No,' started Heath, but his interruption was ignored.

'If you love me Lorcan. Truly, would do anything to keep me safe. If you are my brother, then you will carry her back for me.'

Lorcan stood pinned to the ground, a suffocating scream trapped in his chest. He thought his head would explode, but instead a tear traced silently down his cheek matching the torment etched deeply across Foster's face.

'Do this one last thing for me brother,' whispered Foster, his mouth dry, his lips sticking together at the edges, 'And I promise, I will save her.'

Lorcan felt his knees buckle. He knotted his fingers around his head and swallowed the nausea gripping his throat. His fists clenched with tension as he let the space tighten around him. Silence clawed at him, broken only by the solitary howl of a wolf.

… And then one foot slowly after the other … Never taking his eyes from Foster's own watery, hollow stare … Lorcan took the last few steps into the water.

Chapter 9

Ava sat motionless in Cedric's kitchen, unaware of Lorcan's impossible decision in Daron. She watched the cream swirl into the black coffee in front of her and wondered if Cedric had added anything mystical to the cup.

'I've ruined everything,' she whispered, staring at the table for fear she would cry. 'I'm sorry Cedric. Perhaps you didn't choose so well.' She couldn't raise her eyes to meet him.

'You think I chose you?' replied Cedric, surprised at how little Ava seemed to understand.

'None of it matters now,' she continued, ignoring his raised eyebrows, 'I am just Ava. I didn't cause a fuss before, and I won't again. I was never special.'

'You need to stop this,' he stated, proudly. He would have got angry, but that was no longer his way. 'Nothing is ruined. You are not ruined. You are changed.' He sat down opposite her at the table and stared intently. 'Did you think you would go through this life and not be changed?'

Ava looked up, 'Of course not,' she shot back, annoyed at how flippant he seemed to be. 'But look what it's cost me. I lost Sean, whoever he may have been,' Ava sighed, as one tear rolled down her face. 'And Grace.'

'That is in your hands to change Ava, not the universe,' interrupted Cedric. 'It is your choice not to see Grace, not hers.'

Ava looked away, back to the coffee.

'Everyone grows,' continued Cedric. 'From each trial, each joy. You have a choice in which direction.'

'Sorcha didn't have a choice,' whispered Ava.

'And so you intend to give up?' Cedric had never counted on this from her.

Ava shrugged her shoulders.

'She did have a choice,' stated Cedric forcefully. Ava saw the coffee shudder from the force of his voice. 'And she knew what she wanted. She never doubted herself, or you for that matter. Ever. How many girls did you rescue? How many, Ava?'

'Twelve.' It was a quiet reply, but Ava shivered.

'Twelve,' repeated Cedric. 'So few, in such a vast sea of ruined lives. But, to each of those twelve, you changed their world. Completely changed their world, Ava. Their destiny. And to the Fae that love those twelve, you changed their lives too. And to each Fae that hears of you, that raised a hand to help you. You gave each of them hope. You showed a new way to be, to stand up and be counted, make a difference. Even to those that believe you and Sorcha are just a story, you have given them something to believe in.'

'That was then. Now Sorcha's dead, I can't carry on.'

'Why? You think she would sit here and give up, if you had died?'

'That's not fair.'

'Life is not always fair Ava. Make her death mean something. You can't change it, but you can honour it.' Cedric grabbed Ava's hand. A tingle sped up through her arm. 'Do not allow her to die for nothing. Find your place in their world, Ava.'

'I don't know how.' Ava's voice sounded fraught, but Cedric was pleased it finally had more fight lacing through it.

'Then work it out,' shot back Cedric, his tone still unrelenting, 'Accept help where it is offered and stand up for what you want.'

Silence hung between them.

'Can death be changed?' Ava searched Cedric's face.

'I don't understand your question.'

'You said her death can't be changed. But, can she come back? What I mean is, can we bring her back?'

Cedric studied Ava. He still gripped her hand, and he felt a coldness creep across his fingers.

'No.'

'Really? It's just that...'

'Just. What?' Cedric cut across Ava harshly. His tone so strange to her, she abruptly closed her mouth and stared at him.

A moment passed where neither spoke, but a dull ache growing behind Cedric's eyes compelled him to swallow his dread and speak again. 'There was rumoured to be a dark, unstable power thousands of years ago.' He wasn't sure how much to say, but he didn't want to keep anything from Ava. The kitchen had turned damp and unwelcoming and Cedric noticed a darkness thickening outside his windows, watching and looking for a way in. 'A potion was talked of. Made from the crushed skull of a human baby, freshly killed blue lizards and fresh water toads. Wrapped and dried in sea worms, and then sprinkled with poison from the liver of puffer fish. A complicated concoction.'

Rain lashed against the window now, large droplets as if the lake of Daron had been blown apart.

'But it was just folklore. Without the ancient words, the long buried incantation, any potion that existed would be useless.' As Cedric spoke, his stomach lurched over. The smell of magic filled the air. It twisted around the human cottage pushing objects over and sinking into the very crevices that Cedric had kept human for decades.

Ava jumped up, startled by doors flying open. An icy wind picked up her cup and smashed the china, smearing hot liquid against the wall. Cedric stared around the room with growing horror. He had never felt such an empty, coldness in his bones.

'Please tell me this is not true.' shouted Cedric, 'Who has done this?' Anger saturated his words. 'Ava,' his voice was piercing, 'If you care anything for all our futures, Stranger or Fae, you will tell me now. Who has done this?'

Silence fell. The wind dropped. The rain no longer stormed the windows.

Foster walked into the kitchen, with Jess cradled in his arms. 'I did,' he said quietly, staring directly at Ava.

Just beyond him, Ava could see Lorcan. His hair dripping water down a bruised chest. His newly acquired wounds gaping open and rivulets of blood covering his stomach.

'Oh Foster,' Carter's cocky voice flowed past Lorcan, almost knocking him down, 'Let's not take all the credit now. Where would you be, without me?'

Carter stepped into the kitchen and smirked at Cedric's horrified expression.

'Carraeir?'

'Hello, dearest old man,' smiled Carter. 'You don't look so pleased to see me.' He pouted his bottom lip, feigning sadness, and then threw Ava a glare. 'But then I see you've replaced me. You certainly have a weakness for our kind. Us poor half-Fae's, never quite fitting in.'

Chapter 10

'What have you done?'

The anguish in Cedric's voice bled out across the room.

'Here we stand, old man,' started Carter, his posture defiant, but his eyes holding on to Cedric like a child. 'The three of us in one room. The children that never quite belonged. And in the absence of love and belonging, there will always be suffering, no matter how hard you choose to pretend otherwise.'

'Then you have learnt nothing.' Cedric threw the words back with a power Ava had never felt from him before. The air around them blurred as if time was suspended.

'You are a child of the universe, Carraeir,' he bellowed, 'You are no less than the trees, or the stars. You have every right to belong, and you had all the love you needed to make it so.' He moved towards Carter now, with a gaze that burnt, 'I am sorry that you feel no peace, but you cannot fathom the consequences of what you have done.'

'Do not call me Carraeir. My name is Carter,' he answered, but he resisted the urge to shout into Cedric's face.

Ava inhaled cautiously, as if to breathe too quickly would ignite the air around her. She tried to follow Foster's expression without moving her eyes. She knew he was as stunned at the revelation as she was. Carter was half-Fae. Surely this was good news. The thought was immediately swallowed by the overwhelming truth that Jess was no longer in the lake. Caught in Foster's arms, she looked angelic and far to stunning for someone who had died. Ava's legs buckled.

'Don't you see Ava?' said Carter, catching her arm, 'We are the same.'

Ava lifted her head and stared into the clearness of Carter's eyes. So blue, so childlike.

'You, me, and Foster. We don't have to force ourselves to fit in where we don't belong. Together we can make our own family. The Fae and the Strangers, they will bow to us. We will be the best of both worlds.'

Ava noticed Lorcan scoff. At least she assumed that's what

he was attempting to do through his pain. Cedric had moved towards him, and they seemed to be communicating wordlessly. It also occurred to Ava that Cedric had made no attempt to touch Jess's body. As she pulled her focus back to Carter, a fierce resolve surged through her.

'Answer me something,' Her voice was taut, 'Did you know who Foster was, in Kahors, did you know? Did you plot all along to befriend him? Did you send the information that made Lorcan go to Kahors? Was it always part of your plan to get Jess?'

'I leave nothing to chance,' was the only blank answer Ava got.

'In some ways you are right, Carter,' she finished, 'Like you, I will not force myself to fit in. I will have the best of all worlds. 'But,' Ava's voice turned steely, 'Make no mistake. We are not the same.'

*

Clusters of Fae gathered around the villages and dwellings of Daron. A few were baffled or intrigued by the thundering sounds they heard coming from the lake, but most whispered with a sense of apprehension. But as they looked at the mist swirling, and gathering pace towards the Stranger's lands, none could deny their fear. The ground was covered with golden Rana frogs desperate to leave the edge of the water, now frothing and spewing out silver carp and blue trout. Overhead, Osprey jostled for space as they swooped in and had their fill. Some villagers whispered of the men they had seen arguing. All were fearful of the threat from the other realms. It was impossible to believe, as some gossiped, that Lorcan and Foster were caught up in the commotion.

'I do not believe this place is safer than my chambers right now.' Lilliana weaved amongst the crowds, her head bowed and her face concealed in a scarf made from plain silk. 'I think we should return to the castle.'

'Just hold tightly to my hand and keep walking,' answered Brennan. He didn't look at Lilliana as she complained, and he didn't stop moving. Her hands and arms were bare on his insistence that she wear simple clothes to blend in, and he could not recall a time when their skin had touched for so long.

'Listen to them, Brennan,' she blurted out, as they picked up their pace to avoid a collection of spooked deer coursing along the path, 'They have no appetite for war. They have heard of my plans to heal Daron. I am popular. Do you hear them?'

'Keep your voice down,' retorted Brennan roughly, 'All I need right now is for you to be recognised.' He still smarted from watching Lilliana's intimacy with Foster. He knew his feelings were foolish. From now on he resolved to simply do his duty, which, for now, meant keeping the leader of Daron alive.

They moved in silence, heads bowed, in harmony with one another's steps. To the villagers they were a young couple in love, fingers entwined, arms close, rushing to get somewhere.

Brennan halted. He could hear pounding, but the air hung thick with a violet mist and it was impossible to see where the noise was coming from. His mind spiralled. What was happening? Where was Lorcan? Why had Foster returned?

'Brennan?' The whimper from Lilliana jolted him back. He needed to think quickly. 'Brennan. Look!'

Lilliana had never seen so many creatures move together with such speed. They forced the mist out of their way, surging forward with a power that shook the ground and rattled the windows of the simple cottages nestled along the hillside. Wolves forged with deer, followed by cattle. Overhead, birds of prey overtook, ignoring the weaker creatures at the back of the stampede.

'Something not of this world has taken place,' muttered Brennan, as he searched for an exit from the rampaging animals now coming at them head on. 'And now the universe demands we pay,' he breathed, and with one unwieldy tug he launched himself and Lilliana through the small wooden door of the nearest hut.

*

'Enough,' blasted Cedric, startling everyone. Only Lorcan seemed to fade slightly at the sound of the old man's voice. He sunk towards a chair.

'Lorcan,' continued Cedric, 'I have felt your resolve and your pain. I know you believe you owe Foster everything, but this is a step too far. He has asked a high price of you. You both believed in your own fairytale and we will all pay with our blood.'

'Come on, Foster,' interrupted Carter, 'I knew this was a mistake. I knew the old man would never help us. Let's take Jess out of here. I know some people in town that will give us shelter until she recovers.'

'Recovers?' shot Cedric, and once again Ava jumped, not used to his anger or the fear she saw in his eyes. 'You think Jess will recover? You think this creature is anything like the girl that sacrificed herself?'

'What do you mean?' asked Foster, wanting to put Jess down, but not trusting anyone around him.

'Don't listen to him, my friend,' added Carter.

'Don't call me friend,' spat Foster, turning on Carter. 'All I wanted was Jess back. All I want now is to leave this place and be with her. That's all I want. My only family now, is Jess.'

'No,' winced Lorcan, 'You can't leave. You are my brother. We are family.'

Cedric and Ava exchanged glances, watching Lorcan's pained expression as he spoke.

'I've had enough,' said an aggravated Carter, lunging towards Jess, still unconscious in Foster's arms. 'Give her to me.'

As Ava and Lorcan both lurched towards where Foster stood, the air crackled and froze around them. They could hear it breathing as it turned to ice. Through the blur of cold they watched as the space where Foster had stood with Jess faded. The colours bled away until only a misty hue remained. They had gone.

'Cedric, undo this now,' screamed Lorcan, pushing at the air, which seemed to yield to his touch, only to push back with the same force.

'I must have time to think,' retorted Cedric. 'This cannot be allowed to play out.'

A sudden rip of fire tore down the centre of the room. Ava turned in time to see the heat stream from Carter's fingers, burning his arms and contorting his face. 'Your time for telling me what to do was over long ago,' he hissed, freeing himself from Cedric's constraint and disappearing.

As the final swirls of ice faded, only three remained.

Cedric looked frail, thought Ava. For the first time in her life she saw how old his soul really was. And Lorcan, he could barely lift his head to look at her.

'What should I do now?' she asked quietly. Ava thought she should feel afraid, but in truth she was oddly empty, as if she was waiting to decide who to be.

As if he could read her mind, Cedric spoke.

'You may not have always known you were different Ava, but now is the time to finally accept what you were born to be. You are part of the Fae. There can be no more pretending. Your life was forever changed when Annie died, and you need to accept all that has been, and make it part of you. Keep walking forward, with all the scars you carry. Make them count for something. Do not run away from this.'

Ava drank in Cedric's words, reminded of something Sorcha had said to her, not long after they'd met.

'I cannot change what has been, but I can feel the scar. I need to feel the scar, always, and keep walking forward.'

She gave Cedric the slightest nod of the head as she walked over to Lorcan.

'Take my hand,' she instructed as she pulled him to standing, pressing herself against his bloodied side to support him.

'Where are we going?' he asked without much protest.

Ava felt him lean into her as she wrapped her fingers around his. 'We're going home.'

'Home?'

'Yes, to Daron.'

*

Lilliana could still feel Brennan's fingers digging into her shoulders. She could feel her heart thumping inside her ribs. But now, as she took the longest breath. She felt safe. As impossible as it was, with chaos screaming down outside, she felt secure in the tiny space.

'I apologise,' whispered Brennan, and it made her shiver. She was under him, pinned down where they'd stumbled. She knew the floor beneath her was hard, but instead she focussed on his breathing as his chest pushed against hers.

'Why?' she asked, not really caring what the answer would be.

'I appear to have thrown you on the floor, in some kind of storage shed,' continued Brennan, keeping his voice low, but lifting his head to look directly into Lilliana's eyes. The smell of bread and coffee wafted around them, but Brennan focussed on the aroma of almonds, knowing it came from her hair.

'I see now why you have no partner, Brennan,' teased

Lilliana, her lips curling in enjoyment despite her efforts to look unamused. 'You should perhaps come to me, for advice, in future when you wish to impress a lady.' Brennan allowed himself a smile, and let his eyes wander across Lilliana's face and down to her throat. Her hands tightened across his back.

'We should stay here, at least a while longer, until I can check it is safe outside.'

'Do you think this is the work of armies from other realms?' Lilliana felt hot from Brennan's gaze, but equally she was desperate to keep his eyes on her.

'I don't know,' Brennan's voice was soft, his breath swept across her throat. He felt her shiver as he locked her gaze to his.

'But I believe only the Elders in each realm still see the profit in war,' he continued, trying to keep his voice steady. His thighs pushed against hers, their stomachs taut. Despite the layers of fabric between them he knew she could feel them fusing. 'For most Fae, war is a cowardly distraction from the real problems of peace. I believe you are right. The Fae, your Fae, want to heal. They want to be worshipped as they believe the universe intended.'

As Brennan spoke his gaze moved to spy through the cracks in the wooden door. He could see very little, despite the continuing commotion outside. Lilliana felt the absence of his gaze like a pang of grief.

'Should I marry?' she blurted out, 'What I mean is,' she

added, when he pinned her with a sharp green stare, 'Do you believe it would help the Fae to take me seriously as their leader? If I take a man and behave as my predecessors have?'

Without thinking, Brennan traced his thumb down her cheek. A slow sad smile lifted his face. 'You have no predecessor,' he drawled, 'You are one of a kind.' The silence was consuming, blazing between them, until he spoke again, 'I meant what I said before. You should marry who you please, when you please. My father would say, that we need a new manner of thinking. To survive we need to adapt. Besides,' he added, the smile now growing broadly, 'I pity the man who tries.'

'Tries to what?' interrupted Lilliana, with a mock look of exasperation.

*

Foster had followed Cedric's silent instruction, knowing he wouldn't be followed if he moved quickly. Jess seemed weightless in his arms, but he supposed that was just the adrenaline coursing through him. He smiled. Since discovering he was only half Fae he'd wondered how many traits of the Strangers he carried. When he'd realised there was a way to bring Jess back, the revelation of his humanity had bothered him less. He'd decided it would only bring them closer. If he was less Fae, and Jess now more powerful, he surmised, they could live happily for longer without him draining her human spirit; the price for loving him.

As he kicked open the door of the cottage, he looked at it with fresh eyes. Placing Jess gently across the bed, his stomach lurched to his throat. This was *his* mother's home. This had been his home, until Kallan had ripped him away. He tried to remember playing here, but the memories were so vague they could have been from a story book. He ran his hand across the shelves, piled with books and candles, searching for a familiar reflection. Nothing came. He supposed this was Ava's cottage now, and he was glad. He wondered if they would have to leave Ava, in order to live in peace. He hoped not, but he was prepared to sacrifice everyone now for Jess. He smiled, rolling her name across his head.

'I will love you for all of time,' he whispered against her hair as he lay down next to her, 'I will hold you as high as the stars.'

The irony that Heath, his father, had probably said the very same thing to Annie, on this bed, crashed into him. Just for a second, his resolve faltered. But then he remembered. He wanted no part of the Fae life. Heath was no-one to him, and he refused to be sucked into the Fae world ever again.

'Foster?' Jess's voice was a confused murmur.

'I'm here,' Foster said softly against her cheek. 'I'll always be here. Just you and me Jess.'

As Foster took Jess in his arms, he felt the familiar tingle through the air between them. He felt a strength surge across his belly as if she made him indestructible.

'Do you promise?' she asked, searching out his mouth with her own.

'I promise.'

'I want you,' she breathed against his lips, moving her body against him.

'I'm yours,' was all he could say.

*

Brennan knew he had been staring at Lilliana for too long, but he couldn't tear his eyes from hers. The yellow burnt so vividly, it hurt to look at her. He saw a fire there that transfixed him. Too painful to look, more painful to break away.

'Tries to what?' she repeated, but her voice was soft, as if she actually wanted his opinion.

He moved his hand into her hair, and shivered as the silky red curls wound around his fingers. 'I pity the man who tries to tame you,' he whispered. 'I do not believe you should obey any man.'

'Not even you, Brennan?' she asked, a teasing smile curling one side of her mouth.

'Especially not me,' he answered, and before he could stop himself his mouth came down on her. He could feel the punch of Lilliana's heart against his chest as she pulled him deeper against her. She kissed him back with a passion that confused them both. Brennan pulled away first, aware that his body was aching for her, and sure at any moment she would command him to leave. Their faces hovered, almost touching, the air between them warm and intense. Brennan moved his hand down her arm and on to her hip, tracing a line across her belly and down. He couldn't stop himself and he wondered why Lilliana hadn't. She sighed as his hand rested across her thigh. She pushed herself against him, arching her head back as his mouth moved down her throat.

'I cannot protect you like this,' said Brennan, his words a whisper against her skin.

Lilliana pulled his face back to hers, 'Then, do not protect me,' she replied as she pressed her lips against his.

*

The sun was rising on Daron when Ava set Lorcan down on the cushions in his chambers. It had been some time since Ava had been here, but she blushed as she remembered. His bed had dominated the room then, as it did now, and she avoided it still. The cushions and throws across the floor looked identical; soft, velvety, deep reds, and silky dark purples. Ofcourse they did. Who would change them? The thought of Lorcan with someone else made Ava sting, but she pushed it aside as he winced.

'Do you have something I can use to soothe these wounds?' she asked gently, moving the sodden hair from his face as he laid down.

Lorcan touched her hand, placing his fingers along hers on his face.

'Why are you helping me?' he asked simply. His eyes were black, but they held her gaze with interest.

'Because you're an idiot,' retorted Ava, enjoying the chance to berate him, and trying to pull away from his stare. 'And because you need help,' she added more kindly.

'In the box over there,' said Lorcan, pointing to an ornately carved dresser fitted to one corner of the room. 'Open the drawers and you'll find salves with turmeric and horse chestnut.' Lorcan paused, waiting until Ava had turned away, 'I know I made the wrong decision,' he admitted.

Ava returned, placing several glass bottles by his side. 'I'll get water and clean towels,' she said quietly, feeling his gaze follow her across the room. It made her shiver, but she hoped he wouldn't look away.

'I wonder what's more painful,' said Ava, as she knelt to

undo Lorcan's shirt. He watched as she unbuttoned his clothes. He trembled from fatigue and the pain of wounds that refused to stay closed. 'These injuries, or you admitting you were wrong,' she finished with a triumphant smile.

Lorcan didn't reply. He watched Ava carefully peel layers of bloodied bandage away and clean his chest and stomach. The feel of her hands working across his body made him ache for her and confusion tore through him. He knew she was angry with him, but, still - she stayed.

'What if Jess is just Jess?' he said slowly, 'What if Cedric is wrong and Jess is unharmed?'

'I have seen many things in the last year, Lorcan,' replied Ava, not looking up, or moving her hands from him. 'But I have never seen Cedric angry before. Never. This is not over.' The muscles across his stomach tensed under her fingers. Ava blushed and quickly reached for the salves.

'How do I do this?' she asked, hesitating, but aware she would have to touch him again.

He took her fingers, now smothered with the contents of the bottles and guided her hands across his body. Ava was reminded of the time Lorcan had danced with her, guiding her body with his. The intimacy of the moment made the room blur until all she could see was the darkness of his stare. All she could feel was the skin covering a wall of muscle beneath her finger tips.

'Why are you really helping me?' he asked gently, not

letting go of her fingers.

'Because,' she answered, meeting his eyes and letting his fingers trace over hers, 'I have never felt good enough. I have never known my place in the world. And I still don't.' She winced at her own honesty in front of the one person she thought would mock her. 'But I know here, with the Fae, I will find my place. I am determined.'

When Lorcan didn't come back with a smart comment, Ava looked at their hands, resting together, 'And we have so much to put right.'

He had never heard her say 'we' before. It implied she was with him in some way, and his body ached for her again.

'Will the salve heal the wounds?'

'From the lake perhaps.' Lorcan spoke gently, wishing more wounds on himself if it meant he would feel Ava's fingers on his skin. 'But not the wounds from Kahors. I must bear those for longer. The magic inflicted was ancient and vicious.'

Feeling exhausted, he lay back amongst the cushions and closed his eyes.

It was growing dark outside when Lorcan woke up. He wondered how many hours had passed. He could hear Ava breathing, and feel the warmth of her arm resting across him. The rest of his body felt cold. Leaning across he traced his hand down her shoulder and felt her shiver. He pulled at a velvet throw and covered them both. He watched her sleep until his eyes dragged themselves closed. He dreamt he had the courage to take her in his arms and love her.

*

Both Daron and Blair slept deeply that night.

The calm before the storm.

Except for Cedric - He paced around his cottage. Sometimes he started towards Daron, but never made it beyond the village green. He thought about waking Maria, but the burden felt too heavy. Fog was rolling in fierce waves from beyond the forest, and he knew for sure Foster had taken Jess to the cottage. Carter had unleashed a plague, and Cedric felt fear soak through his bones.

And Jess – She woke screaming. Dreams of drowning gave way to visions of herself tearing at the flesh of the people she loved. Her body was decorated with the hearts and hands of her victims, and each suffocating step she took to reach Foster was fused with agonising burning.

'Jess.' Foster shouted, pulling at her arm to wake her.

She screamed until it was soundless.

And then she stared at Foster.

Her eyes were the colour of blood …

And in them, Foster saw ruin and sorrow.

Chapter 11

Maria smiled as she carefully placed chairs around her pretty patio tables. Last night had been unusually cold for this time of year, and now she gazed towards the low sun, wondering if Autumn was coming early. She loved the Autumn here. The smell of the leaves and the burnt earth, becoming damp and ready for harvest. The deep colours; seductive and earnest. But mainly she loved it because it was the only time the Strangers truly noticed their world. They saw the colours change, they commented on the fall of the leaves, they laughed at the squirrels saving for the winter. It made Maria feel at home. It made her believe there was hope for everyone.

But this morning, there was something new. The low sun

may not have been unusual, but the birds remained in the trees on the village green, despite the enticing wiggle of the worms along the dew. The grass was iced with frost in places where the sun couldn't reach, and a flurry of fog seemed to lay in wait just beyond the trees.

Carter watched Maria's joy as a young girl waved on her way past the café. An intuitive smile flitted across his mouth when Maria called out to the girl that she'd be welcome to pop in later, and bring her brother, for hot chocolate and cookies.

'Am I welcome too?'

His voice made Maria spin violently. Words caught in her throat as her stomach twisted with elation and apprehension.

'Carraeir?,' she stumbled, sitting in a chair as her legs gave way, 'It can't be?'

'Carter,' he said kindly, pulling a seat opposite her and taking her hands, 'I go by the name Carter now.'

She had longed for this moment since the day he'd left, but she'd resigned herself to believing he would never return. Now, he was almost unrecognisable. He had grown taller, leaner, and his face seemed beaten and older than his years. But, there was no mistaking the cornflower blue of his eyes, and the smile of the cheeky, unsure boy he had once been.

'Where have you been?' she asked gently, running her hand

down his face and holding it there. She wanted to throw her arms around him, but she stayed paralysed with shock.

'All over the place,' he replied softly, leaning his face to her hand. 'I have seen so many things.' He placed his own hand over hers to stop it leaving his face. It was warm, despite the cold air, and she smelt of fresh dough and cinnamon.

'And,' Maria's voice wobbled with emotion she had buried, 'Did you find what you were looking for?'

Carter stared at the woman who had loved him since he was a small child. The woman who had carried him home when he'd been abandoned. She hadn't cared where he came from, and she'd never wondered why no one wanted him. She had just loved him. Simply that. Made him her son, and loved him.

'I hurt you,' he said simply, not answering her question. He had never said it before, and he found it stung more than he expected. 'My leaving, it was never about you though, you know that don't you?'

'I know I wasn't enough,' Maria stumbled, not wanting to make Carter feel sorrow for her, but knowing there was no point lying to him or herself any longer. Too much time had passed.

'I didn't know who I was. That's all. I thought one day I would fit in. One day I could stop feeling second best.'

'You were the only one who cared where you came from.'

Maria struggled with the words as tears warmed her face. 'I tried so hard to teach you your beginnings were unimportant.'

'I know,' he said quietly. 'I am sorry I hurt you. You have loved me and I wish I knew how to repay you. I fear I will only bring you more sorrow. Perhaps you should have left me alone that night. Let the wolves take me.'

'No.' Maria grabbed at Carter's hands and held them to her face. 'Do not speak that way. There is nothing that cannot be undone. There is nothing so bad that we cannot start again and be a family.'

'I'm not so sure,' he replied, wanting to believe Maria, wanting to feel her hold him like a child again.

'I will always love you Carr..Carter. You are my son.'

Maria pulled Carter to her and kissed his forehead. She wrapped her arms around him and silently thanked the universe for returning him to her.

Carter relaxed into her embrace, letting her tears fall down his cheeks. He felt safe and he wanted it to last. He wanted the only mother he had known to hold him tight against the chill, but as he closed his eyes all he could see was regret and shame; All he could feel was loathing for everyone around him.

Everyone, except Maria.

And he knew, it was too late.

It had gone too far, and it could never be undone.

*

'I can feel something bad within me Foster.'

'No. We have come too far, and I will not let anything happen to you.' Foster pulled Jess against him, stroking her hair and letting the warmth of their bodies distract him from the desperation in her voice.

'Foster, you're not listening to me.' Jess's voice was fragile. Foster closed his eyes, willing himself to hear her heart beat. 'Nothing bad will happen to me. That's the point.'

Foster held her closer. He ran his hand down her spine, taking pleasure from the way she trembled and pushed against him.

'You're not making any sense,' he whispered into her hair as he eased her body under his.

'Nothing bad will happen to me, because I am the bad,' continued Jess, struggling to control the desire to give in to Foster again.

'Let's stay here,' he murmured, delighting in the heat of

their nakedness, 'Just one more hour, and then we will seek out Cedric. The old man will have calmed down. His storm can't last forever.'

As a fevered passion consumed Foster and Jess, the usually solitary Muntjac herded out from the safety of the forest. Chaperoned by Buzzards, they hurtled away from the cottage towards the village green, agitated and formidable. Jess closed her eyes and let go of the need to talk. A smile crept slowly to her crazed eyes, and when she spoke, only the creatures of the forest heard her.

'I am the storm.'

*

Carter marched across the green to the man waiting on the bridge. He pulled his jacket closer to his body. The sun was climbing but the air was stubbornly cold.

'This is not where we agreed to meet,' he hissed, checking back to make sure Maria had gone inside the café.

'We grow impatient for our delivery.'

Carter sighed heavily. He had to admit he hadn't thought this part of the plan through, and juggling the neediness of The Order, and Heath and Raisa, and now Foster was boring him. Double crossing the lot of them should be easier than this, he thought as he turned to leave.

'Where do you think you're going.' The man lunged at Carter and gripped his arm. 'You promised us a weapon. It is The Order's destiny to finish the Fae. If you don't deliver by this evening, you will have the might of our organisation upon you. You will watch your family die, and then they will finish you.'

'I have no family,' spat Carter, fixing his eyes on the man, knowing he could slice his heart out here. 'There is nothing you can do to me, that I have not already done to myself,' he finished, pulling his arm sharply from the man's grasp, and deciding the kill would be too easily seen in such an open space.

The man watched Carter striding towards the forest, away from the village green. But he also watched the petite red head who owned the café smile towards Carter even though he couldn't see her. He saw how she stood and watched him disappear. He smirked as she lingered outside, long after Carter was gone from view. Maria, that was her name, he remembered. He looked at his watch and saw that it was late morning now.

'Time for lunch', he said to himself, as he headed towards the café.

*

As Ava woke up, a cold but shrill sunlight was piercing through the windows. Her sleep had been deep. As her brain caught up with her body, she jumped, remembering where she was. Lorcan had slept next to her. The thought made her inhale sharply.

'I let you sleep,' came his voice. He sounded preoccupied, and Ava wondered if he was embarrassed.

'You were up early?' she asked. 'I hope it wasn't me that disturbed you.'

Lorcan looked at Ava, contemplating what to say. He wanted to tell her she always disturbed him. Distracted, mesmerised, captivated. It was all disturbing, but instead he said, 'We have a problem.'

Ava rose, running her fingers through her hair. Lorcan knew she was trying to make herself look tidy but he had enjoyed looking at her this morning with chaotic hair and a peaceful expression.

'What's happening?' exclaimed Ava, now staring out the window alongside where Lorcan stood, 'Who are they?'

'Elders from other realms,' replied Lorcan heavily, 'And soldiers.'

Ava stared at the groups of Fae dotted on the furthest side of the lake, extending back towards the edges of Daron's lands.

'Why are they here?' Her voice was a whisper.

'Because everyone felt it,' said Lorcan, after a sigh of resignation, 'We have ripped through the balance of nature, and the ripples are felt across all the realms. Some will be here to seek guidance, some will already know what we have done. They all seek to own it.'

'It,' fumed Ava, 'You mean Jess. She has a name. And what's with the *we* all of a sudden. You did this. You, Foster and Carter.'

Lorcan sighed, heavier this time. They had been so peaceful last night, Together, bonded. Now they were arguing again. And, Lorcan knew he had news to deliver that would alienate Ava even further.

'Yes, you are right,' he began, 'But you are here, with me, right now. And as such you must decide if you wish to return to Blair, or stay and help. A meeting must be called with my sister. And Foster, and Carter if we can find him. And now Heath. All of us must be accountable.'

Lorcan winced as Ava's face swung round to his.

'Heath?'

'Yes.'

'My father?'

'Yes.'

'Alive?'

'Yes.'

The silence was stormy, as their eyes bored into one another. Finally Ava found her breath. It juddered through her chest.

'Take me to him.'

*

Lilliana stood on her balcony and smoothed down the simple chiffon layers of her dress coat. She craned her neck to watch the gathering huddles of Fae, mindful that Brennan would not want anyone to know she was back in the castle. Brennan. The thought of him sent an exquisite shiver spiralling around her stomach. And then she remembered how quickly he had become a soldier again as they'd left the village and caught sight of the congregating Elders and their entourage. She felt hurt, then anger, and then something new to her, concern. She wondered where he was now, and more than that, she worried that when she saw him again, he would want to be nothing more than the soldier.

*

'Was it all really so terrible that you couldn't get past your beginnings?'

Cedric had waited in the clearing in Blair, knowing Carter would try and pass to Daron soon.

'Out of my way, old man,' replied Carter, but he stopped short of reaching for his blade. 'What is it you want from me?' he challenged. He stopped walking and stood close to Cedric, he towered over the former Elder, but he felt no malice towards him.

'I wonder now, would you prefer to have been lied to? Would it have been better to hide the truth from you and raise you in a human family?'

Carter remained silent and stared at Cedric.

'You were loved. Maria wanted you, protected and raised you as her own. She never defined you by your beginning, so it pains me to see that you do, Carter.'

'And you think I should be more grateful?' Carter raised an eyebrow.

'No,' Cedric touched Carter's arm now, and Carter felt a familiar warmth float through him. It reminded him of ball games, and evenings by the fire reading with Maria. Comforting human activities, only ever spiced kindly by Maria with the knowledge that he was special and could do great things. 'No one is asking for your gratitude,' Cedric continued to speak kindly, 'But it pains me that none of you are happy, none of you can find peace.'

Carter closed his eyes, reflecting on the path he had chosen, Cedric's hand still burning comfort and calm in equal measure.

'Foster and Ava,' continued Cedric, 'Half Fae, separated and lied to their entire lives. Lorcan, abused by privileged parents. Lilliana, well, where do I start,' he smiled, as he thought about the changes Brennan had talked of. 'But you, Carter, of all of them it was you that had balance, love, and honesty. I wish I knew what exactly you need to feel peace. To be at peace with who you are.'

'I need…chaos.'

Carter was stunned at his own honesty. He pulled his arm away from Cedric, scowling, wondering if he had been tricked with magic.

'Chaos?' repeated Cedric.

Carter felt weary. Suddenly he didn't care for the game of sneaking around. The deed was done anyway. Jess was back and growing more powerful by the hour. There was no going back, chaos was inevitable.

'Yes. Chaos,' Carter answered calmly. 'You see, I'm not on anyone's side. I don't belong on anyone's side. Heath thinks I am helping him regain power and the love of his children. Raisa thinks only of that same power. Foster, well he just wants to feel love. And then there's The Order,' Carter smiled now, 'They are perhaps the biggest fools of all to trust me. They pay a handsome price for a weapon against the Fae. And, that's what she is, a weapon. They are all fools to think you can bring someone back from the dead and control the consequences. That is their vanity. It is not mine. I do not serve any of them. I have used them all. Taken a little piece from each of them, and created chaos. Last night, there was a magical hue across all of the worlds. Calmness and a need for love. But like a tsunami drags the water back before it strikes, soon they will see that Jess is not for owning. They will bow down to her power, or die trying.'

'Why?' Cedric's eyes filled with tears for the lost little boy in front of him.

'Because,' Carter looked straight at Cedric, his own eyes holding his tortured soul, 'In the middle of so much chaos, I might close my eyes and feel the calm.'

*

'Does she really have to be here?' Lilliana tossed her loose curls back with one hand as she stepped completely from the balcony. She refused to make eye contact with Ava.

'I think we have bigger problems, Lilli,' retorted Lorcan, striding fully into the room with Ava and Brennan behind him.

Lilliana noticed the half smile Brennan gave Ava. She felt a whack of envy in her chest.

'We should at least listen,' said Brennan, moving closer to Lilliana and moving a lone stray curl from her face. She nodded, but all she could think about was the way his finger lifted her hair. He'd heard reports in the morning that villagers believed themselves to be under an enchantment the previous night, and he wondered if Lilliana was now regretting their closeness. He searched her eyes.

Lorcan raised an eyebrow at Ava.

'Tell us what you know.' Lilliana's voice was sharp and high, a defiant attempt to regain control and not look anything less than a leader.

The room remained silent except for the calm of Lorcan's voice.

Ava winced as he recounted how he had met Carter and the injuries he had suffered in his quest for Foster. He didn't tell Lilliana the punishment was because Ava had dared to rescue Fae, and she loved him a little for that. Loved him. She sighed heavily as she acknowledged the inconvenient truth.

Brennan huffed loudly as Lorcan retold what he now knew about Carter's role in events. His instinct had been right, and he clenched at the knife strapped to his thigh wishing he could march out of the castle and slice Carter's throat.

But it was Lilliana that sat quietly, sinking further down in her chair as her brother spoke of Foster. It seemed inconceivable that funny, playful Foster would use such powerful magic. Would bring someone back from the dead. How was that possible? It sounded grotesque and the air around Lilliana grew thinner until she thought she might pass out. Only the news that Heath was alive snapped her back to Lorcan.

'So Foster wants his rightful place after all?' she questioned, looking from her brother to Brennan, a deep line between her brows.

'No,' said Lorcan abruptly. 'All Foster wants is to take Jess and live away from the Fae.' His voice trailed the last words with sadness. 'But I cannot speak for Heath,' he rallied, 'To believe Carter, would be to believe Heath wants power. And he will harness Jess and use her to defeat us all.'

'But Heath says he only wanted Foster's happiness?' interrupted Ava, not sure why she was defending the Fae she had never met.

'And you believe him?' asked Brennan.

'Of course she doesn't,' Lilliana snorted. 'I know that look, and she's got more sense than to believe the smooth words of a man who so casually ignored her for an entire childhood.'

The two women locked eyes in silence for several seconds.

It would seem the only common ground they found, was their inferior fathers. The irony stung.

'And what about Jess?' Ava blurted out the words, wanting to slice the connection with Lilliana, and determined to make Jess the priority.

'That is why I wanted us together,' replied Lorcan, his eyes like ink as he looked at each of them in turn. 'So there can be no argument.'

Ava felt tension burn through her shoulders and chest, fearing the words he might be about to say. 'No,' was all she could manage before Lorcan spoke again.

'Cedric is right. Whatever Jess is, she cannot be allowed to remain.' He took a deep breath, forcing himself to look at Ava. And the loathing and anguish he saw in her eyes was acid on his soul.

'But she hasn't done any harm,' retorted Ava, 'What if you are wrong? What if Cedric is wrong? You keep saying she is bad, but she has done nothing to hurt you. Any of you.'

Lorcan would have given anything to agree with Ava, but instead he replied, 'She hasn't done any harm, yet, Ava. And when have you ever known Cedric to be wrong? We cannot afford to wait.'

'How could anyone agree to this?' Ava looked around the room, but no one spoke. 'Who would be so hard-hearted, so callous? You can't find her guilty before she has committed any crime?'

Lorcan took a deep breath, ignoring Ava's words, and when he exhaled, his chest felt heavy. 'I brought her out of the lake, so it must be me who returns her.'

'I can't believe I'm hearing this,' interrupted Ava, storming towards the door.

He closed his eyes. 'It must be me who finishes this.'

*

Cedric had stood in silence for too long. As he struggled with the enormity of Carter's actions he could only see the young boy he had found here in the forest.

'And what if you die while you stand calmly amid this chaos?' he asked, knowing the answer before it was spoken. 'What of Maria's son then?'

'Then I shall be returned to the heart of the universe.' Carter smiled sadly. 'Perhaps it is too late for me, Cedric. But, if I am to have one regret, it is that I could not be a better son.'

Cedric returned his hand to Carter's arm.

'I know Maria deserved more.' Carter's words were a whisper.

'Come back with me, please. There is always an answer. Always a different path.'

Carter wanted to believe Cedric. He was about to place his hand over the old man's when a flurry of wings from a pine tree took their attention to the edge of the clearing. They stood rooted as the man Carter had met earlier came striding towards them, dragging Maria by her arm. He pulled her in front of him and placed a long knife against her throat.

'No family? Or just more lies?' he boomed, spittle lacing the edges of his dry mouth. 'Not even this one, Carter?' He pushed the blade against Maria's skin and Carter saw it redden as blood traced where the edges grazed her neck.

'You wouldn't dare,' roared Carter, as he sprinted across the clearing.

'You promised a delivery, and this is your warning. Do not mess with The Order.' The knife was lifted ready to plunge into Maria's chest.

Carter screamed, 'Wait!' as he launched himself at the knife.

His fingers almost reached. Almost got there before the blade was thrust down. Propelled with such force, Carter thought he heard the sound of Maria's heart break open. As he wrestled her murderer to the ground and sliced his throat with ease, he didn't take his eyes from the only person who had truly known him.

Known him.

Loved him.

Maria's empty eyes stared back as her life spilled and sank into the dirt.

Chapter 12

In the days that followed, Autumn seeped in to each of their lives.

Foster and Jess made the cottage that once belonged to Annie their own Eden. They devoured each other with blind exclusion to the world outside. To them, the walls took root in the forest, the last of the summer warmth melted the windows, they no longer knew if they were free or prisoners to an unstoppable fate. Only the moments before sunrise muted their passion. In those seconds, they would sit silently, their nakedness covered only with silk throws, and marvel at the resilience of the morning. Jess would smile at Foster and stroke the face she loved so deeply, knowing a time was coming when she would be consumed with the need to sabotage all the beauty. She would raze her own happiness. Crush and dismantle the very love that she held in her hands.

She knew it was true, even if Foster didn't believe her capable. She tore her eyes from him, as she did every morning, and looked towards the creatures of the forest that ventured bravely each sunrise towards them. Those that caught the edge of her gaze whimpered and bowed. Some howled, and fled as if scorched by her stare. But she knew, when she concentrated, when she focussed the poison inside her body, that deeper in the forest, the creatures that she caught by surprise, simply dropped down dead.

She knew it was true because she felt the light go out in each soul .. and, she felt her own steadily wither.

*

Lilliana shivered and raised the green velvet hood on her gown over her hair. She pulled at the curls, making them fall like red silk down to her waist. She wasn't cold, but Brennan's eyes taunted her. The dress reached the floor and covered her hands, and though she knew it skimmed like a glove, it gave her comfort that Brennan could see nothing of her. She didn't want him to know her body was on fire, that she ached to feel him touch her again. Each day was the same. They waited together, wondered when she should approach and address the growing crowd. She no longer knew what she was waiting for.

Finally, after days of glances and little conversation, she snapped.

'I grow tired of waiting for Lorcan. I plan to address the crowd.' Her voice was sharp.

Brennan watched her move across the room. The colours she wore and the fire in her spirit took his breath away. A symphony of everything Autumn. As a child he had often wished he could fly. Travel the worlds, chasing the seasons to watch the trees turn to their most glorious. But now, he wanted nothing more than to be with her.

'This enchantment you mentioned,' her voice stayed sharp, precise and prickly, but she waited for his reaction to the words before she continued, 'The one that made people do absurd things.' Her stomach rolled as Brennan lifted one eyebrow at her, 'Do you think it's over? Do you think there will be some sense amongst the crowds if I address them now?'

She knew that wasn't really the question she wanted to ask. If an enchantment had really proceeded the ruin they were all facing, then the passion she had shared with him wasn't real. And it was over. And the one thing she was certain of – was that she didn't want it to be over. Lilliana cursed under her breath. Brennan hadn't answered her unspoken question and more than that, she needed to focus. This was not the time to let a man distract her.

'Answer me,' she shouted sharply, 'If I wanted a dumb

animal to look after me, I would invite the wolves in.'

Brennan's head jolted. He could feel the hurt searing through his face, but he tensed to cover his reaction.

'I think you should do whatever you feel is best,' he answered carefully, torn between duty and injury.

Lilliana lowered her gaze. She fiddled with the sides of her hood. It could have been annoyance, it could have been regret. Brennan couldn't tell, and he knew she would never apologise

'But, as for the wolves,' he said firmly, as he reached the door, 'They are loyal, strong and work as a family. You would be wise to learn from them,' he added cryptically, his glare holding her. 'Learn to share their spirit. There are worse things you could do than invite in a wolf, Lilliana.'

*

Someone who had embraced the wolves was Ava. Or rather, they had embraced her. Now, as she lay on a patch of lilac clover, two females joined her. She had felt their approach, heard the softness of their pads on the earth. It no longer startled her. Even when she felt the damp noses explore her cheek and eyes she simply smiled. They had settled beside her, backs turned, heads rested on their front legs. Ava couldn't see if their eyes were open, or if they slept alongside her. She wished Lorcan could see this, he would surely be impressed. Lorcan. Ava stared at the pure pink and tangerine colours falling from the trees above her. Everything about Daron was saturated with him. All the colour and passion she found here, all the complexity and sharpness … she saw it all when she looked in his face, when she watched him walk, when she listened to him talk. It was maddening.

'Am I disturbing you?' Lorcan's voice wafted over her before she saw his shadow across the moss.

Ava sat up. She watched as his eyebrows wrinkled, causing a deep rut to form above his nose, but his eyes didn't seem so black. She was still angry with him, and he sensed it.

He offered his hand to Ava, and without thinking she took it, letting him pull her up from the ground. Their skin fizzed as they touched.

'I have come to ask for your help.'

Ava remained quiet, but didn't let go of his hand.

'Before I,' Lorcan faltered, Ava felt his hand tighten around hers. 'Before Jess returned, Carter left something for me.' The words tumbled out then. 'An incantation as old and powerful as the magic used to inflict these wounds.' He lifted Ava's hand and placed it against his stomach as he spoke.

'Why would he help you?'

'I don't know. Perhaps he thought it would buy my loyalty.'

'Or perhaps he just feels alone.'

Lorcan looked quizzically at Ava.

'The words,' he said, 'They need to be spoken together by a Fae and a half Fae. Perhaps he intended me to ask him. When the incantation was created the Elders of Kahors would have never believed a half Fae would be accepted by our kind. It would have been an empty promise of healing. The last laugh, you might say.'

Ava realised she was pressing her hand against Lorcan, and he made no attempt to move.

'Will you help me? I know a place along the river bank where the water is purest, running straight from the mountains. If I take you there now, will you help me?'

Ava stared at Lorcan's eyes. She was trapped by a desperation in his voice.

'Yes.'

*

Carter had no idea how many days he'd spent wandering from realm to realm. In fact, he had crossed from Blair to

Daron so often, he sometimes woke to find he couldn't remember which side he was on. The irony amused him. He was, ofcourse, alone and it didn't matter where he was. Or who he was. He had no side. It had never mattered to anyone who he was. He was no-one. But, he wanted to be important. He wanted to be noticed. And then, he would replay the horror... Maria dying. And that torture, of knowing he had mattered to someone, would slice him again. The truth was he was important, he was different, and he had thrown it all away. The thoughts spread like poison until he could have ripped his own heart out with loathing. He drank. Wine, infused with narcotic herbs dulled the pain. Numbed him to the point where he felt detached, where the misery couldn't find him. Numbed him, so he felt nothing at all.

*

'Daron is full of the most absurd places,' remarked Ava as she stared at the cave Lorcan had brought her to.

The walls were covered in mosses that blazed. Thick blankets of pinks and burnt oranges made the walls and floor look like velvet. The trickle of water tracing a path down the back wall, to a sparkling puddle of diamonds gave off an impossible light.

'Just because something is absurd, does not make it untrue.' Lorcan pulled Ava close to the trickle of water as he spoke. Ava contemplated his words, realising he was right.

'Place your hand over the water, let it blend with your skin,' he instructed, breathing the words against her face.

Ava did as he asked, letting him cover her hand with his, pressing against the wall of the cave.

'I need to remove the bandages,' he said.

Ava's eyes moved to his chest and the t-shirt that covered him.

'Lift your arms,' she said gently, staying close to him and pulling the fabric up and over his head. He watched her as she unwound the bloodied bandages. When she was done, she looked up and stared at him, only inches away from her.

'What now?'

He took her hand again and pressed it against the water. Droplets ran down their arms, tickling and teasing at their skin.

'When you are ready, trace your fingers across me. Let the water run against the skin, into my wounds. Feel the water as it touches me.'

Lorcan's voice was a whisper, deep and penetrating as she did what he asked.

'Keep going and whatever words you hear me speak, repeat them.'

Ava felt the cave melt against her as she started to methodically run her fingers lightly against Lorcan's chest and stomach. She felt his muscles tighten at her touch. With each stroke of water his breathing quickened, and she found herself whispering words against his ear as she followed his lead. The walls of the cave became a sparkling aqua silk undulating against the trickle of water, consuming all sense. Ava had no idea how long they stood there. She couldn't tell if the words were being said out loud, or just running through their minds in tune with the cave breathing. Lorcan knew they didn't need to stand this close. He could feel the sting of the wounds knitting messily together, he knew it would leave scars. He knew he should move away from Ava, the healing was complete, but the heat from her hands was addictive. Each touch was like molten wax.

'Do you wonder,' he breathed against her hair, 'Why people spoke of sorcery and bewitchment the night Jess returned, but we were together and unaffected?'

Ava had wondered exactly that, over and over.

'Perhaps your stubbornness outwits even the fiercest enchantment,' murmured Ava. She could feel Lorcan's smile in her hair as his mouth moved against her.

'Or perhaps your sharp wit and sarcasm convinces the universe to abandon all hope.'

Ava lifted her head, astonished to hear humour in his voice, and to tell him the wounds looked untidy, but they had stopped bleeding. She bit her lip as their faces touched. Lorcan could feel her breath in his mouth. He pushed his hands through Ava's hair and pressed closer to her. She let their lips touch softly. Neither moved. They breathed against each other savouring the feeling of each other's skin, listening to the punch of their own hearts.

'I want to kiss you,' she couldn't believe what she was saying.

His teeth grazed her lip, 'What will the universe say about that?'

He had never felt so utterly consumed. Joy and agony swirled with an aching adoration. Ava felt one hand slide defiantly down her back while the other fiercely crumpled her hair, and then as if she had commanded it - his mouth covered hers.

*

The sun gave Carter no warmth as he approached the cottage that had once belonged to Annie. It was Ava's now he mused. Ava, who seemed to walk between worlds as easily as stepping through a brook. He pulled up the collar on his jacket as the forest sunk a little further towards the night. He had fleetingly wondered if meeting other half Fae would help him belong, but the thoughts had never really reached any surface of his being where they could attach and grow. His foot crunched across branches on the floor of the forest edge and a flurry of bats raced deeper into the trees.

'Hello.'

Her voice made Carter snap his head up towards the cottage. A whoosh of buzzing light flooded from the trees.

'Hello,' he replied carefully, walking slowly towards the porch. He had to concentrate his focus as thousands of shining insects swarmed around the cottage until it seemed covered in jewels. A burst of late sunlight illuminated the tangerine leaves strewn on the porch. They blazed like torchlight against the dusk.

Jess sat and calmly waited for Carter to reach her. She didn't seem afraid or perturbed at all that he was in the clearing around the cottage. She sensed his turmoil and regret.

'I'm Jess,' she said steadily, and the words seemed strange, as if she had said them before, differently, in another lifetime.

'Carter,' he replied, realising that she didn't recognise him. Why would she? She hadn't been conscious when Lorcan had carried her from the lake.

'Are you alone?' asked Carter. He wasn't sure why it mattered, he had no plan right now. But he was used to being in control, it was a habit.

'Foster is asleep inside,' she replied with no agenda, 'I came out to watch the sun set on another day. The Fae taught the first Strangers that the sun sets to remind us that endings can be beautiful.'

Jess wondered how she knew that. It was as if she'd always thought it, but she knew that couldn't be possible. Carter stared at the fading light, mottled with cloud and punctured by the tree line.

'They also say it brings a promise – of the dawn.' He found the way she looked at him oddly comforting.

'Do you look forward to the new dawn, Carter?' Her voice was kind, but synthetic. She knew she wanted to know the answer, but it would make no difference to her.

Carter thought about the question for several seconds. Jess didn't take her eyes from him. He looked sad.

'Perhaps,' he finally answered. 'It might be nice to walk into a new day, and be, different.'

'Tell me how you would be different.' As she spoke Jess felt tears on her face and she noticed that Carter stared at her. She couldn't see the blaze of red cloaking her eyes, but she could feel the power envelop her again. She sensed the creatures of the forest shivering in anticipation, so she clasped her hands tightly together as if she didn't trust herself.

'All my life, I always had to out perform everyone,' Carter

found himself compelled to speak, and, even though the words were truthful, it brought a physical pain to hear them. 'I wanted to over achieve, to be perfect. I was demanding and cruel to myself, but no matter how well I did, I never felt it was good enough. I always needed something more.' Carter paused, noticing Jess's hands twitch. Howls came from the trees, and the shining insects extinguished like candles, one by one falling to the floor.

'I never found my calm in the chaos,' he finished quietly, 'I never found peace.'

'Chaos,' echoed Jess, now smiling and lifting her hands up in surrender. More howls sang out mournfully and the moon dimmed behind a cloud. 'Do not be afraid to step into the morning, Carter,' she smiled serenely, but Carter's stomach lurched. 'Because the morning will bring panic and fear. A beautiful chaos.'

'What do you plan to do?' he asked, watching the emerging moon highlight the fury in Jess's eyes.

'Everything,' she replied forcefully, 'And nothing.'

Jess pinned him now with eyes that blazed triumphant, but pitifully sad.

'For some, Carter, it will never be about finding calm. The storm doesn't have to lead to peace.'

'What?' Carter felt the air harden between them. It crackled as it froze.

'Death sits and watches me. It has no eyes to see, but it waits, wondering my next move.'

'Jess! What are you talking about?' Carter squinted trying to focus on Jess, 'What will happen in the morning?'

'This ending *will* be beautiful.'

Chapter 13

'Wouldn't go back in there just yet Mister, too many wolves prowling close to the oak on the other side.'

Carter was startled to see a young girl leaning against the ancient archway.

'What? Who are you?'

'You're heading to Daron, right? Through here?' she touched the stones gently.

'Um, yes,' replied Carter, trying to make sense of the child who could be no more than six. She was dressed like a Stranger, but as he studied her, her long dark waves and aqua eyes gave off a distinct Fae aura. As the morning sun moved higher, lone rays seeped through the trees and bathed her in peach light, and it hit Carter that he had seen her before. At the café. In a school uniform. She was the girl Maria had called out to. 'Bring your brother,' she had said, for hot chocolate and cookies. Carter studied the girl.

'I just got back,' she continued innocently, 'Which side do you live on? I live here, but I'm allowed to visit my Gramme Fae once every full moon. Mama will be here in a minute to meet me. She's a bit late.'

Carter crouched down, staring.

'Wait. So you are Fae?'

'Yes,' stated the little girl, looking quizzically at Carter. 'My name is Tabbris. Mama says it means, very determined. But Raz calls me Tabby cos it's easier to say.'

The little girl showed no fear and Carter smiled at how easily she shared her information.

'Raz?'

'Yes, he's my little brother. It's Raziel really, as Mama said it was a beautiful mystery that she found love again. Raz's Daddy isn't really my Daddy, but we love each other, and that means we're gonna live happily ever after.'

'And, Tabby, are you all Fae?' Carter was intrigued. The little girl seemed to exude an acceptance and peace that had always eluded him.

Tabbris giggled. 'No, silly. We are a rainbow family. Me and Mama are Fae, Raz is half and half, because Daddy was a Stranger.'

'Was, a Stranger?' asked Carter, now sitting animated on the floor with Tabbris.

'Yes,' she answered earnestly, 'Because it's a silly word, and he's not a Stranger to me. I love him. He's like a Daddy should be.'

'And it's never bothered you? Being different?' Carter's voice was kind. He really wanted to know.

'I'm not different.' Tabbris put her hands on her hips, and frowned, but it quickly softened back to a smile.

'I didn't mean to be rude,' offered Carter, smiling back.

'It doesn't bother me,' said Tabbris, 'Mama says if people think it's wrong, that's their problem. Mama always says, let's not make it our problem.'

Carter rose to his feet. He wanted to stay and chat to the little girl, he liked her, but he didn't relish her mother finding him here, 'May you never change, Tabby,' he said as he started to walk away. 'I am glad to have met you.'

'Are you coming back?' she called hopefully.

Carter wasn't sure what to reply. He had no idea what waited for him on the other side. No idea what was in store for any of them now Jess's new power had finally overwhelmed her. He looked sadly back at Tabby as the air thickened inside the archway. He could see she was calling something to him, but between worlds he couldn't hear.

'Next time, come and meet the others,' she had sang, 'There's lots just like me, and you. We can all cross together next time, in case the scary wolves are still there.'

Chapter 14

Carter knew, as soon as his feet touched the steps, that Daron was waiting for Jess. The sky blazed violet with scarlet clouds descending low across the lake. Creatures that would normally roam and graze, hid away from the damp air. A low hum filled every space, different chants and words of reverence sung so quietly, so constant, that Carter closed his eyes and let the desperate purity of the moment consume him.

'Our actions have had consequences, Carter. Which one of us is the bigger fool?'

Carter's head snapped to attention. He stared at Heath.

'Didn't think I'd see you again,' Carter said plainly, 'It must be obvious to you now, that I never planned to help you become leader again.' Carter wanted to laugh at Heath for being so trusting, but right now that didn't seem so important. 'Suppose you can't wait to tell me, this,' he motioned to the sky, 'Is all my fault.'

Heath took a deep breath. His exhale seemed to last seconds, and he looked weary. 'We are all responsible for the choices, and decisions we make,' he replied calmly, 'Not just you, Carter. If I merely blame you, I would be avoiding the truth about myself.'

'And what's that?'

'I wanted it all back,' Heath replied, moving towards Carter, 'A long time ago, I wanted everything I'd once had. But in my heart I knew my time was over. I loved Annie with every fragment of the universe I could harness, and when I lost her, I lost it all. I take responsibility for my actions, as Jess will hers.'

'I have seen her,' Carter changed the subject, not wanting to contemplate the madness of motives running through his head, 'Jess, I mean. I've seen her.'

Heath had seen her too. But he kept the information to himself. 'And is she everything you hoped for?' He couldn't resist the sarcasm. He lifted his hands encouraging Carter to look around. Pulling the leather glove from his hand, Heath let the water drizzle around his fingers. He could feel the sizzle of powerful magic sting as it seeped under his nails.

'Yes,' replied Carter simply, with no enthusiasm. 'She is turmoil and confusion. She is lawless and free. And,' he took a deep breath, 'She is on her way here.'

'Then I must say goodbye, Carter.' Heath nodded his head as he spoke, but his attention was already in the distance, watching a defiant Raisa striding against the wind. Catching the low cloud, she stretched and amplified the water it contained until it resembled a living beast.

'None of us know what is next for us,' he said, his eyes never leaving Raisa's form, 'I have my peace to make, as I'm sure do you.'

Without thinking Carter bowed his head to Heath. The merest movement, but the most respectful action Carter could ever remember making.

*

Ava wished she was still in the cave. She wanted to keep her hands against Lorcan's bare skin. To feel his fingers pulling at her hair. She wanted his body to stay pressed against her. Her lips felt bruised. She pressed them together desperate for the memory to stay sharp. His breathing was the only sound she wanted to hear, his mouth the only taste she needed. But they both knew they couldn't stay. The noise of madness had carried from the village like a rolling wave, and the darkness had descended so quickly the cave became like a floodlight in the dead of night.

They had walked silently towards the lake, holding hands until they saw the gathered villagers. The invisible strands of passion crackled in the space between them. Each time Lorcan brushed against her through the crowd, she allowed a small smile, knowing his dark eyes were on her. Sometimes she glanced at him and saw how heavily he breathed. She wanted to close her eyes and remember his words. Words spoken into her skin.

'I can no longer tear myself away from you. When I look at you, I burn.'

She shivered at the memory. A delicious icy thrill that stayed in her spine.

'I don't know what will become of us,' he had said quietly, but his hands had betrayed him as he'd lifted her and pushed her closer to the water. 'We can never be together.'

Ava stopped walking now, remembering the passion of his kiss as soon as he had uttered the words. She had held his face and let water stream through their lips filling their mouths with a magic she knew she would never feel with anyone else.

'Ava?' He said her name slowly. She was no longer shocked that his voice was in her head when his lips stayed still.

'Ava, we have to keep moving.'

She nodded, and held out her hand for him.

His eyes dropped, and Ava felt her heart twist as he turned and carried on through the crowd without her.

*

'Do you suppose this is how it ends?' Raisa carried the sides of her billowing gown as she sauntered towards Heath. The palest greys melted effortlessly into pinks and greens. From a distance she fluttered like a serene butterfly against the swirling mist.

'It would be fitting, don't you think?' replied Heath, with a humour that Raisa remembered from a lifetime ago.

'And how is that?'

'You and me. Thinking we were controlling the game. Thinking we could control each other. But, here we are. We have been played, Raisa.' Heath smiled gently. It would always mean more to Raisa to come out on top, and for that he felt sad for her.

'It's not over,' she said defiantly. The gold metal woven through the bodice of her dress held her caged and rigid. 'I will command the lake to take out my enemies. The water will strike down whoever I wish.'

Heath exhaled slowly and chewed at his lip.

'Raisa, stop and listen to yourself. And listen to me,' he spoke with a kindness that made her hold her breath. He took her hands in his and kissed them gently, 'You and I have come so far, lost so much, caused so much pain. For what? Glory? Possessions? Power? And in the end, it might very well be that all we have left is each other.'

Raisa stayed silent. The fog enclosed them, silently whispering memories.

'Starting again is not a bad choice,' he squeezed her hands tightly, 'Start something better. Make a new ending.'

'Where?' Raisa replied, 'Everything I am is here.'

'Would it be so hard to step through that tree. Just for a while perhaps. Live a simple life until the chaos subsides.'

Raisa snatched her hands back. 'Through the tree? You want me to walk amongst...'

'You forget your beginnings,' snapped Heath, seeing a familiar flash of arrogance in Raisa's yellow eyes.

'I will not go back to being poor. I will not walk unnoticed through the crowds. I have sacrificed so much to be… this,' she raised her hands, and mist swirled thickly through her fingers, 'You would have me give up my position for...'

'For me,' interjected Heath. 'You don't have to love me,'

he said kindly, his eyes searching hers, 'You don't have to be with me. You just have to come with me, for now, and together we will find our way. Our ending does not have to be full of anger and resentment. There is power to be had by looking beyond our own walls. Fulfilment to be found in new adventures. We may have the power to begin our world again. We would have a place with Cedric until...'

'Madness,' shouted Raisa, starting to gather her skirts to stride away. The air between them crackled as heavy cloud rolled navy against the speckled night.

'You saved me once, Raisa,' shouted Heath, 'Let me save you.'

As Raisa turned away, she let go of the dress feeling it billow at her will, like wings open wide against the elements. She fought the twisting of her mouth, a silent adamant order to herself not to cry. When the tears cut at her cheeks she told herself the wind was sharp. With every obstinate step she forced herself away from the truth, that she wanted to leave with Heath. She wanted to turn and run back to him. Take a chance. Start again. But pride poured into her bones like cement. Was she destined to let men dictate to her? She deserved to be admired here, in Daron. But, if she did leave with Heath, it would be her choice. And, Heath would grow to adore her. Raisa fought with herself. With every unbending stride taking her further from him, she ached to turn around.

*

'Ava.'

Ava's head shot round with surprise.

'What do you want Carter?'

Carter moved from the crowd to stand in front of Ava.

'Your father,' started Carter, 'He's just over there with Raisa. Have you thought what you will say to him?'

'And why is that your concern?' Ava looked beyond Carter's shoulders, trying to catch a glimpse of the man she had heard Annie talk of. A fantasy that could light the flowers of the night and make them glow until dawn. She realised she was searching just as steadily for Lorcan.

'They killed Maria.' The words tumbled from Carter the way grief steam rolls over any normal moment. 'The Order. They killed her.'

Ava gasped. She wanted to sink down, but the ice in her legs kept her upright.

'Why?' she whispered against the thick pain building in her throat.

'Because I loved her.' Carter bowed his head and Ava felt compelled to lean towards him, 'She was the only person I truly loved. The only person I couldn't stand to lose. The only person who truly loved me.'

'But you left her?'

'Because it was so perfect. So warm. And I belonged.'

Ava bowed her head and cried quietly. Carter's pain was burning from every pore.

'I don't understand.'

'It was everything someone could ever want. And I couldn't stand the waiting. I couldn't live another day wondering, is this the day it will be snatched away from me? The day someone rips it all to pieces.'

'So you decided to end it yourself?' Ava questioned, her eyes saturated with sorrow. 'Rather than live in joy, and work at being happy?'

'I could control the end you see. Break her heart. And mine. But at least it was my choice. No one took it from me. And I didn't have the agony of waiting.'

'But you didn't control it, did you?' Ava wanted to sound kind, she was trying to comprehend the loathing and pain coursing through Carter's soul, but the words came out too fast.

'I don't need you to point the blame at me, Ava. Don't you think I know that?' Carter's eyes flashed bitter and angry. 'Nobody helped me. I didn't have the perfect little start in life you did.'

'Yes you did, Carter,' retorted Ava. 'How is this anyone else's fault?'

'The one person I couldn't stand to lose. Gone.'

'So do something different,' stated Ava getting agitated. She wanted to get moving.

'Easy for you to say, when you have all this,' he gestured to the chaos around them, 'And I have no one, and nothing.'

'Carter,' pleaded Ava, 'Let someone help you. Before it's too late.'

'It's already too late,' stated Carter, looking squarely at Ava. 'Jess will be here at sunrise, and with her comes the storm.'

'We don't have time for this now, Carter. We need to work together. We need a plan.' Ava was getting desperate.

'Would you help me?' His question was simple and asked plainly.

Ava hesitated. She looked behind Carter and saw Lorcan striding towards a woman that could only be Raisa.

'Yes,' she mumbled no longer looking at Carter.

And there at the edge of the meadow, alone, stood a tall man, his coat nearly reaching the floor, his hair unruly, but Ava knew with no doubt it was her father. As he turned and fixed her with eyes so dark she couldn't blink, his mouth lifted in a small smile.

'Despite what I have done?' ventured Carter, already knowing Ava wasn't listening to him.

'Ofcourse,' she replied distracted, more tears soaking her cheeks as her eyes crinkled returning Heath's smile.

'Ofcourse,' repeated Carter sadly, bowing his head in the smallest movement towards Ava.

Stories of Annie and Heath swirled around Ava's mind as Heath turned to face her fully. She watched him start to walk towards her, as if in slow motion, his long strides bringing them closer together for the first time. As she watched him, she knew why Annie had loved him. The closer he got, the more she knew she wanted to know him.

Carter started to move, and with each stride away from Ava, he felt torment. The pain of losing Maria. The sting of not being noticed. The ache of never fitting in. He fought it. He knew there had to be more. He wanted something else. He wanted to stop and let the moment pass. Be rational. And then he remembered Maria's body slumped in his arms and a convulsive sickness raged through his body.

Ava felt hope. The sunrise didn't seem so final. She and Foster would find a way to breathe, to succeed. Be a family. As Carter came back into view, nearly as tall as Heath, with his arms stretched out in greeting, she felt a newness that he too might learn to exist with them. In peace. There was always hope.

Carter walked with confidence towards Heath. He lifted his arms and smiled. He felt no tether to anyone here. He felt no tether to anyone, anywhere. He would be happy to be taken by the storm. His fingers bent down to touch the button on his wrist strap. Blades, perfectly silver, new, shot forward and he squeezed them comfortingly.

Let the storm come, he thought. Let Jess take them all down. Let her wipe away their families. He would control this moment. He would start the madness. He would lead them from hope to anarchy. After all, he remembered, it's not always about the calm.

*

'Carter!' Ava screamed his name over and over. She ran, focussed on the blades, now protruding like arms. 'Stop,' she yelled, until the noise was a frenzied banshee scream.

*

'Just let me talk to her,' Heath stood firm as Carter reached him. 'Just let me hear her voice. Just once. Let her remember me.'

As the blades sliced Heath's chest, a perfect cross through his heart, he didn't take his eyes from Ava. He wanted her to know he had loved her. So many things he would never get to say.

'No,' was all Carter said, as he swiftly removed the blades and carried on walking, his hands covered in blood.

*

Raisa turned and sank to her knees as she listened to Ava's screams. She knew. She saw loss crawling towards her. And she felt a pure horror, knowing it was about to rip at her. Raw, bloody. As her skirts trailed in dirt, she dug her manicured fingers deep into the earth, felt it squelch under her nails. As she lifted her head, the howl of her heartbreak echoed out to the village, causing the lake to shudder and rise with her. Every hidden creature and frightened villager lifted their head to stare.

Chapter 15

Brennan pulled up the collar on his coat.

'I'm going down there,' he stated.

Lilliana bristled. She was still reeling from Brennan's last outburst. The tone of his words blistered her.

'You would be wise to learn from the wolves. Learn to share their spirit. There are worse things you could do than invite in a wolf, Lilliana.'

No one spoke to her like that. No one. How dare Brennan think he could? Fleetingly, she had wondered if she deserved his criticism. But the thought had been quickly replaced with indignation.

'If I can get through, I plan to get to my… to Cedric.' He waited for a response, but none came, 'I know he will never return to Daron, but if we have any hope now, it will lie with him.'

This wasn't how he wanted to say goodbye. He wondered if Lilliana realised there was a chance he might not make it back.

'I am torn,' he decided to say, 'My duty is to protect you. To stay. But I am a useless pair of hands here. I am more used to battle.'

Still Lilliana said nothing.

'I need to run with the pack,' he finished quietly, and Lilliana closed her eyes, hating the new sensation of shame.

'If I wanted a dumb animal to look after me, I would invite the wolves in.'

She knew she had hurt him. She'd never mastered sensitivity, and she burnt not knowing how to behave.

Brennan didn't look back as he marched across the court yard. He couldn't contemplate the agony of never seeing her again, but he couldn't let her know. He was a soldier, and should never have imagined himself equal to her. And in truth, he argued with himself, the best hope of a solution did not lie within the castle walls.

'I need to run with the pack.'

Lilliana didn't move as she watched Brennan disappear from view. In fact, she didn't move for several minutes afterwards. She spoke quietly, her lips hardly moving, wishing the words through the navy night towards him.

'Run with the pack, Brennan. Be the wolf. Be the most powerful, relentless creature I will ever know. Never be tamed, and you will be accepted and loved. But, above all... Come back.'

*

Lorcan walked to where blood stained the mossy floor and sat down next to Ava. He didn't speak. He closed his eyes and listened to her quiet sobs, letting each one bathe him in her despair. He wondered if touching her might absorb some of her pain, but he knew it would splinter her perfect privacy.

Unaware of the villagers gathering around them, they sat in painful peace. The mist was still heavy, blurring out the navy sky, but peeps of pink were trying to nudge the darkness away.

Eventually Lorcan spoke, 'Can I show you what we do to honour those we have loved?'

Ava nodded, but didn't take her eyes from Heath's body.

Lorcan left her then, and nodded to the many Fae now building their own memorial behind them. When he returned he carried his shirt in his hands, saturated with water from the lake.

'Hold out your hands,' he said gently.

Ava did as he asked, and let him squeeze the cold water over her fingers. She watched as he did the same to his own hands.

'Now copy me,' he said simply, gently placing his hands around one of Heath's.

Ava watched as the water sparkled between their skin.

'Take his hand Ava,'

Ava took the hand Lorcan had been holding, and watched as he walked around Heath's body to take his other hand. She looked at Lorcan for guidance.

'Hold it gently. Close your eyes and concentrate.'

Ava realised her fingers were sparkling. Heath's hand was warm and she felt a fizzing sensation. She gasped, looking up at Lorcan.

'Don't look at me,' he instructed carefully, 'Close your eyes and feel the colour. The unseen life force. Energy flowing through us all. Share yours, transfer what you want to say, help him to die well.'

Ava listened to Lorcan's words, immersing herself in the warmth of saying goodbye to Heath.

'And in return,' Lorcan's words were a whisper, 'May you know peace and love. And live well.'

Ava bowed her head to Heath's body, never letting go of his hand. She let her tears blend with the water of the lake as she mourned the loss of a man she knew only through Annie's stories.

*

Raisa watched as Daron built their memorial. A tradition as old as she could remember when someone so loved died where they had fallen in battle. Because battle was what this was now. For Raisa anyway.

'Savage,' she hissed, trying desperately to use her hatred for Carter to push the sickness of loss away.

She stayed hidden. She hadn't seen Daron mourn this way for a long time. They certainly didn't for Kallan. Raisa wondered what had happened to his body. When she'd recovered from the drugs Brennan used on her, she was back in Daron, away from the ground in Blair where Kallan had died. It occurred to her that she had not stopped to mourn her husband at all. And the thought of that, and the grief surging through her body now, made her sob without control.

*

The night turned indigo. The sunrise seemed reluctant to break through and, under the half light, the Fae worked tirelessly.

'What are they doing?'

Ava was still sitting with Heath's body, her hands resting carefully on his chest, but her gaze was being pulled to the colourful wigwams appearing all around her. Each was small, with only enough room for one or two people and different herbs were bunched and hanging upside down to form the crown of the tent. Fae were quietly laying blankets and cushions inside each creation, and illuminating the outside with small candles.

'They are honouring your father,' replied Lorcan.

Ava continued to stare. There must be nearly a hundred here already, she thought.

'When someone dies in battle, someone the Fae wish to honour, then we lie with them for several nights,' Lorcan kept talking, looking out proudly as villagers joined Elders to build. 'The Fae believe in the right to die well. To be kept company while we let go of this world. By being here, we help Heath to carry his burdens to the next life. Perhaps convince him to leave some of them behind and free his spirit to travel quickly.'

'And you believe all of this?' Ava asked, genuinely wanting to learn.

'It is what the Fae have always done,' Lorcan said, standing up now. 'And the people loved Heath. Long before you were born, Ava, he was a great leader. These men and woman feel sadness. They thought they had lost him, but now, they have to mourn him all over again.'

'I can understand that,' Ava said quietly, looking up at Lorcan's extended hand.

'They wish to honour him. Knowing all his faults - they will remember him as a good man. I can only hope for such a send off.' Lorcan lowered his gaze as he spoke, but then added quickly, 'We must move now, the brightest, richest fabrics are saved to enclose Heath and we are in their way. Besides, I have something to show you and you must get some rest before morning.'

Ava took Lorcan's hand, immediately shivering at the intimate touch of his skin. She recalled his words earlier that night …

'I don't know what will become of us.'

'We can never be together.'

They had only walked a short distance when Lorcan stopped.

'Here,' he said, showing Ava a wigwam of dark purple velvet, with a huge bouquet of dried lavender hanging upside down at the top.

'It's beautiful,' whispered Ava, looking at the candles surrounding the outside, and the thick lilac and rose coloured blankets inside.

'It has been built for you.' Lorcan let go of Ava's hand and motioned her to go inside, 'The lavender symbolizes their admiration for you, and the white lavender inside is to protect you.'

Ava felt her eyes sting. So much beauty and love, because Heath was dead. It was so unfair.

'You should rest now, we do not know what the morning brings.'

'Where will you go?' Ava tried not to sound desperate that Lorcan had turned to leave.

He didn't speak. In truth, he didn't know where to go next. He knew his mother was watching, and he could never predict her actions. He wondered where Foster was. He needed to catch Carter. He hoped Brennan was with Lilliana. And then there was Jess. He wished he could just crawl inside one of warm spaces the Fae had created.

'Stay with me, Lorcan,' she said quietly. It wasn't a plea, just a simple request. 'Against your better judgement, just stay here, tonight, with me.'

*

Cedric watched the storm rage around the green. He lifted his hands against the beating rain and tried to find some balance. Despite the wind whipping at the stream, forcing the water up onto the grass, its level was higher than Cedric had ever seen. And he had lived in Blair for a very long time. Normally Cedric welcomed the rain, relished feeling the power of it covering his hands and face, but now he only felt cold fear.

'You are too old to stand here. Look at you, you're soaked through.' Toni's kind voice fought through the wind as she approached him.

'I have been old a very long time,' he replied wistfully.

Toni linked her arm through the old man's and lifted her face to the sky.

'She's out of control.'

Cedric patted Toni's hand, 'Yes. She is. I am at a loss to stop her.'

'Will you go to Daron now?'

'No.' Cedric paused to sigh. His chest was heavy and tired with the effort of breathing against the cold air. 'I vowed I would never return. I have caused enough damage for that kingdom.'

Toni took a breath, ready to answer back.

'But,' Cedric interrupted her forcefully, before she could speak, 'Even if I made myself go back. All the power of my being couldn't stop Jess now.'

'Can nothing stop her?'

Cedric was about to answer, his face crumbled with sorrow, but he quickly forced a smile in place when he saw Brennan striding towards him.

'You are always a welcome sight,' he said, covering Brennan's hands with his own. His heart lifted to know at least his son was safe. 'Is Heath with you?'

Brennan searched Cedric's face, wondering how to tell the old man. But Cedric felt the unspoken words. His chest tightened around his heart.

'Carter,' began Brennan.

'I don't need to hear any more,' interrupted Cedric sadly, 'There will be time enough to tell me.' He didn't think he could bear the details. His breathing became shallow.

'Cedric?' Toni's voice was heavy with love and concern.

'I will recover,' said Cedric, not knowing if he would, 'And right now there are Fae who need your help more.' He paused, the immediate reality of the situation flooding over him. He steadied himself, pulling up straighter, 'Heath and I had a plan,' he began, 'He was to gather as many Fae villagers as he could convince to come through tonight. To come to Blair.'

'What?' The surprise in Brennan's voice was matched by the stunned look on Toni's face.

'Not forever. Unless they wanted to stay of course. Just until it was safe to return. Whenever that might be,' and then he added wearily. 'If Jess leaves anything for them to return to, that is.'

Cedric looked into Toni's eyes and smiled gently, 'I know I ask so much of you Atonia. And I cannot promise it will be the last time. But will you help me? Will you find the Fae shelter if they come through?'

Toni knew she would never refuse Cedric. She had come to find him tonight, not just because of the storm, but because she needed his help. The number of children becoming unwell in Blair was now worrying high. But that wasn't why she needed Cedric. Toni knew Fae lived in Blair unnoticed, but she didn't care. She assumed some would settle and perhaps fall in love, although she knew these relationships were doomed. But she wondered if she was the only one that had noticed the increasing numbers.

'Atonia, I can help from Daron if you meet me at the gateway.' Brennan waited for a response. 'Toni? Are you listening?' His voice cut across her free falling thoughts.

There was no time today for her worries, she concluded. She would have to keep them to herself. 'Yes. Sorry. Yes. I'll meet you. I'll sort something out. Bring as many as you can.'

'They may not come tonight,' added Brennan, lowering his gaze from Cedric, 'Tonight, they honour Heath and help him on his journey.'

Everyone heard Cedric breathe in, 'Of course,' he said, nodding his head and trying to stop his lips twisting with despair. 'I am comforted to know that.'

Brennan smiled at Toni, 'I will see you in the morning. Wait for me, but be careful. Jess will take the same route on her way to Daron.' He was about to turn away, and then without thinking he embraced Cedric. 'I think you would be the first to tell others to forgive themselves,' he whispered, 'Do not hide in the shadows. Because without you, the rest of us will indeed flounder. I know I am glad to have found you.'

Toni watched Brennan walk away, and although she didn't want to disturb the moment for Cedric she needed to ask one more thing,

'You didn't get a chance to answer,' she said carefully, 'Before, when I asked if anything can stop Jess. Is there any chance?'

Cedric turned to face Toni and nodded. The lines on his face etched deeper.

'Lorcan.'

*

The meadow where Heath had fallen was illuminated with candles. Raisa silently weaved a path around the wigwams careful not to catch her skirt on the flames. She could sense the love and respect wafting towards the tent where Heath lay. It looked beautiful, larger than all the rest and covered heavily with silk and velvet in the richest hues of blues, until it blended with the lake and night sky. The scent of glory and courage consumed her as she brushed aside the bunches of Bay, and Edelweiss covering the entrance.

And there he was, surrounded by Lavender and covered with Sage.

Raisa gently held her lips against his. She wound her fingers through his hair and swallowed each sob as it wretched from her body.

An hour passed while she poured water from the lake into his wound and whispered every combination of incantation she had ever practised. It was too late, she knew that, and she closed her eyes pressing them to his, wishing she had the courage to take her own life and hope they would be together.

Eventually, she laid in the dirt, and wrapped herself around his dead body.

'Tell me where you are going,' she whispered to him, 'And I will find a way to meet you there.'

*

Ava laid with her eyes closed, but sleep didn't come. She had her back to Lorcan, and as the last of the candles extinguished against the dawn she turned to look at him. As her eyes traced the lines of his nose and mouth, she wondered if they would ever kiss again. She touched his hand, not caring if he woke, and was surprised when he twisted his fingers around hers.

Lorcan opened his eyes and turned his head to Ava. He had listened to her breathe for the last hour. Every time she exhaled he wished he could pull her to him.

'Hold me,' she whispered, easing herself against his side and touching his face.

Lorcan pulled her close to him and wrapped his arms around her. Their faces so close he could feel her lashes against his. His whole body ached for her.

'I've lost so many people, Lorcan.' Ava's lips moved against his cheek and he held her tighter. 'Sometimes I list their names in my head, as if I'm scared I'll stop remembering.'

'That will never happen, Ava,' he replied, letting his lips press on her skin, and wishing her mouth would find his.

'Why did you honour Heath?' asked Ava quietly, 'I mean, I didn't know him, but I wish I had, but you, you had more reasons not to honour him, didn't you?'

Lorcan sighed. He wasn't used to explaining his feelings to anyone. And the more he told Ava, the more he was bound to her.

Ghosts of watery light had started to drift into the small space, Lorcan knew outside the sunrise was about to flood the new day. The new day - perhaps their last day. He smiled softly at the tricks the universe threw at him.

'No,' he replied smiling. 'I had every reason to honour him. I wanted to tell him that Foster is a good man. I wanted to tell him that his people will never forget him. I suppose in some ways I wanted to show him that he was a greater man than my father. Does it matter to me that he might have tried to regain power? Not really.'

Lorcan meant it. When he had left Lilliana to rule, it had been temporary, but now he realised that he had not thought about being leader since he had been back.

'But it's more, Ava. More than the past.'

'What do you mean?' Ava pulled her face away slightly to look into Lorcan's inky eyes.

He smiled sadly, he may as well be honest with her. It was becoming clear to him, their lives were destined to be bound, for better, or for worse.

'I asked Heath to show me his strength. I asked him to show me how to get through the next few hours without losing myself, and the people who mean the most to me.'

Ava ran her finger tips down Lorcan's face. If she kissed him now, she would never hear what he had to say.

'Today Jess will come,' he stated quietly. 'She will march into Daron and she will unleash havoc on my people. She won't be able to stop herself. It won't be her fault. But she must be stopped. Even if that means she needs to die. You know that Ava, don't you?'

'Yes.' It almost wasn't a sound, and in it Lorcan could feel the pain of Ava losing Jess all over again.

'Foster is like my brother. He is my brother. But I do not expect him to forgive me.'

Ava continued to stare. It wasn't as if she didn't already know any of this, but it stung and made her chest raw to be reminded.

'And so you see now, why we can never be together.'

'No, I don't understand,' Ava didn't want to hear any more. And if he said it out loud, she would have to listen.

'You won't want me when this day is through, Ava.'

'Lorcan, stop.'

'It must be me that carries Jess back into the lake.' He held his voice steady. 'If the universe decides it, it will be me that rips out her heart and you lose her a second time. You will look at me, and see the Fae who killed your best friend. I have to live with that. And yet, still I want you. But,' he repeated the words, 'You won't want me when this day is through.'

Ava lent her head back against Lorcan and closed her eyes. She wondered if they were his tears she could feel wetting her face. She remembered something Annie had quoted to her a long time ago. The reason long forgotten, the author never known, but she repeated the words now like a mantra - over and over.

'Courage doesn't always roar. Sometimes courage is the quiet voice at the end of the day, saying, I will try again tomorrow.'

She kept repeating it, until the time came to face the day.

Chapter 16

It was like an upsurge of bedlam as Jess walked from the cottage to the clearing in Blair. The ground undulated under her feet, the earth moved out of her way. She left a rift that froze, marking her path towards the gateway to Daron. A gateway she could now see clearly. She focussed, narrowed her eyes and smiled.

'Move,' she commanded to the men assembled across the clearing. They couldn't see the stone arch, they weren't Fae, but they knew it was there. Carter had told them that much.

'Did you think you could control this?' Jess's voice bellowed, and the bravest birds scattered from the branches.

'Was your plan to own me? To make me kill at your will?'

Some of the men took a step closer to Jess, raising the guns in their hands. A few stepped back, feeling the ice gripping at the air they wanted to breathe.

'I am not afraid of dying.' Her words surged at them, crushing the hands that held guns and forcing them all to their knees. 'Pieces of me are dying all the time.'

Jess's eyes were blank as she lifted her hands towards the men.

'The Order!' she shouted, 'You gave yourself a name, and crowned yourselves in charge. You thought you could capture chaos? Tame her? Make her bend to your will?'

A swell of leaves rose from the ground and scrolled around Jess, cocooning her, turning brighter with orange and red until she looked smothered in flames.

And then, with small flicks of her hands, targeted at each foot soldier… the killing started.

Chapter 17

Carter and Toni watched from different sides of the clearing. Both hidden. Both wondering where Foster was. Neither were foolish enough to stand in Jess's way.

As Jess stepped across the threshold of the stone arch, she shivered with her own strength. She didn't look back at the bodies crumpled where they'd fallen. She didn't see the cracks in the ground where she'd trodden. Her intake of breath as she passed through to Daron was sharp, and fused with thunder that roared across both worlds.

When they stood up it was Carter that spoke first.

'What will you do now? Do you have Fae on the other

side?'

'My life is on this side,' replied Toni without hesitation. 'I will see if any of these men can be helped.' She looked around knowing already there was no life left here, 'And then I will walk back to the village.' She intended to wait for Brennan, see if she could help at least a few Fae, but she wasn't about to tell Carter that.

'What about you?' she asked to deflect his attention away from her plans, 'Do you have Fae in Daron?'

'No,' he replied bluntly, 'There is no one there I care about any longer.' He thought about Lilliana, wondering if Jess would find her. How could she not, he concluded sadly.

'So where will you go?'

Carter paused. It was like the eternal question he had been asking himself his whole life. Where would he go? Where did he belong?

'To Daron, of course,' he answered absently, 'I have no where else to be.'

And as he disappeared into the flurry of space inside the arch, Toni thought she heard him say, 'The chaos is only just starting. Wouldn't want to miss the show.'

Chapter 18

Daron heard the thunderous entrance of Jess. Fae soldiers from Daron and beyond surged towards the steps leading from the Oak. The sky blazed orange, and the air crackled as they raised their weapons.

'There is nothing that can stop me.' Jess spoke without volume, but everyone could hear her. 'You could gather every beast, every Fae, every human. You could gather the souls of those you've lost, and still, nothing will defeat me.'

And, as if to prove her point, Jess moved her gaze to a group of Fae now racing towards her, and snapped their necks with a flick of her wrist.

'You can never control the universe. You don't reason with it. You don't bargain with it. It was here long before you. It has weathered your meddling and considers you insignificant. It has seen civilisations grow and implode. You will not be the last. You are not unique. More arrogance. More greed. More hate. And they will all fail. All of them.'

Lorcan and Ava watched with increasing horror as soldier after soldier fell to the ground. The cracking and popping of their necks, the grinding of their spines breaking.

Ava bent over, convinced she was about to be sick. Her head was dizzy, but she couldn't take her eyes from Jess. Their eyes met for a fleeting second, and Ava was convinced she saw recognition, a spark of hope, but then it was gone.

When the soldiers had stopped falling. Jess turned away and focused on the lake.

'My beautiful home,' she said. 'The beginning of all life, the breath, the calm, the power. I wish you could all taste the water, feel her magic the way I do.'

And then she twisted her hands over and over, rolled her arms in a flurry that caused sparks to ignite the grass around her.

The water rose.

Small at first, so no one noticed, but with each ripple came another, growing wider and fuller, and louder, until a swollen wall of water had risen from the lake like an unfurling monster.

Villagers screamed and ran towards the steps. Many had agreed to leave with Brennan, but now even those who would never contemplate leaving Daron fled towards the Oak.

The water roared, as if it were storming land, but it stayed perfectly static, twice the height of the castle and as dense as a mountain.

'I can't stop this,' bellowed Jess against the noise of the lake. Her voice was fractured and odd.

'Run,' shouted Brennan to the villagers too stunned to move. The mass of water hung like a molten, living sculpture. Too horrific to contemplate, too beautiful to take your eyes from.

'Run'

'She's fighting it.' It was Carter. Now standing at the foot of the steps from the Oak, he stared at Jess. 'She's trying to stop the chaos.'

'Help me, Carter,' Brennan was raging now, 'I don't need much of an excuse to rip your heart out. So help me.'

Carter was about to laugh at Brennan. Laugh at the absurdity of him threatening to kill, when they were all about to die anyway. He wanted to watch. He wanted to see how many would die before Jess controlled the power. If she ever did. He doubted it would be that easy. But then he saw Tabbris.

'Tabby.' He whispered the word to himself.

Still dressed like a Stranger, the long dark waves pulled back in a pony tail, and her unmistakable aqua eyes. His mind instantly recalled the first thing she'd said to him. Innocent and completely accepting of who they both were.

'Wouldn't go back in there just yet mister, too many wolves prowling close to the Oak on the other side.'

'I have to let go,' screamed Jess, 'I have to let go.'

'Tabby,' screamed Carter. He hadn't expected to ever see her again, much less here, in Daron. His stomach lurched, and the feeling unnerved him. His mind raced in circles, wondering if he could reach her. But then what? How could he save her? Why would he save her? What would Maria want him to do? What did he want to do?

The water dropped.

Like a lead weight had fallen from the sky. It crashed so absolutely, sucking the air around it and spitting it back out, that no one had time to seek cover. Those directly underneath its power wouldn't have felt their death. Those in its path would have been broken against the rocks and trees, slammed, nature against nature.

'Tabby?' Carter's shouts were lost in the roar of water.

'Gramme!'

Carter could hear her. It was feint but he remembered that's what she'd said to him,

'I'm allowed to visit my Gramme Fae once every full moon.'

Why did she come back again so soon? 'Tabby!' he yelled again, his chest tight.

'You have done this.' Jess spoke, pointing her finger at Carter. The tip buzzed with power. 'The innocent will die alongside the guilty. That is the price. There is always a price. You think you can command nature? You think you can pervert the natural order of life and death? You crown yourselves Kings and Gods and demand respect? But there are consequences. Always consequences.' And she slowly bent her outstretched finger and flicked it towards a crowd of Fae.

'No! Wait!' screamed Brennan.

But the already crumbling banks collapsed on command, covering the group with water and mud until nothing was left. Carter sank to his knees as he watched Tabby crash against rocks. His body froze as he watched her disappear under the murky water being dragged towards the centre of the lake. Some of the Fae around her were grabbing at moving debris, but he didn't dare hope she was strong enough to cling on.
Anger raged through his chest, and he raised his arms to

eject the knives strapped inside his jacket.

'Make me stop,' called Jess, and she hugged her arms around her head. She could feel the panic and fear of everyone around her. Her body was craving their terror like an addiction. She screamed with revulsion.

And then she saw Ava walking towards her. It was just like all the times before it. She was just a teenager again. And Ava was her best friend.

'It's nearly taken me,' she said quietly, lifting her hands to stop Ava getting any closer. 'I have no choice.'

'I believe you,' replied Ava, her mouth twisting with misery. The burning in her throat made it almost impossible to form the words.

'I want to surrender. I can feel myself dying. And this … whatever it is … will be all that's left. I don't want to be remembered that way.'

'You won't be,' was all Ava managed to say before Jess's eyes burned with a new fury. The space around her fingers twisted and froze, before propelling sheets of icy water towards Ava, forcing her high in the air and slamming her down at the foot of the steps.

Jess screamed with rage as a new heat seared down her side. She felt blood pulsing from her body and knew she'd been stabbed.

'Did that hurt?' yelled Carter, as Jess pulled his knife from her side. She felt the rush of pain as the metal moved inside her.

'Nice try,' she hissed, 'I didn't see you coming. But, you should have learnt by now.' There were sparks flying from her entire body as she moved towards Carter, 'The universe will always remove, what is no longer serving it.'

She twisted her hands, laughing as fire danced around her arms and through her chest. Once again, the waters began to ripple and swell. Not just the lake now, but all the surrounding water full of Fae and debris. It lifted and pulsed like an organ. An entire ecosystem held at Jess's will. Bigger and heavier than the first time, Carter knew if this slammed down on them, there would be nothing left.

'You cannot rearrange the universe,Carter,' she bellowed, and then closing her eyes she whispered, 'Only yourself.'

And then the water fell. Harder, and louder than before. It pounded the ground, and shook the earth. Screaming and cries of despair filled the air. Bodies bashed against each other in crippled confusion. The impact set off a wave of water, as high as the castle, surging across the lands. Ice cold and sharp, it whipped up everything in its path. Like an army of ants it gathered pace and carried the injured and dead as it travelled. It twisted around itself changing colour as it absorbed the earth, speeding away from the new surge Jess planned to unleash.

Still blazing, Jess raised her hands and threw her head back to savour the rush she felt. Her fingers ached, but she knew she couldn't stop.

Lorcan marched solemnly towards Jess. The effort of getting close to her now was exhausting. Every step felt smaller with each renewed push.

Jess watched Lorcan approach, as a pulsing sting replaced the ache in her hands and tightened its way up her arms. She felt the energy drain from her body as the burn of a million tiny needles marched across her chest and down towards her legs.

'Asrai,' announced Lorcan, but he felt no joy. He'd seen Lilliana on the balcony, wondered how she could ignore the carnage below her. He'd felt a disappointment and anger that she stood aloof from her people in their time of need. And then shame, when he'd realised she was using the small piece of the lake she could command to summon their help. He stood about twenty paces from Jess allowing the Asrai to swarm fluidly around her. He wondered where Ava was, and then immediately hoped she couldn't see him.

'What are they doing?' asked Jess, her eyes still blazing, but her body crumpling as the Asrai clung to her, covering her like bandages.

'Absorbing the energy you make,' said Lorcan, 'Harnessing the natural acoustic waves, reacting against you, forcing the energy to spread differently.'

Jess only growled, a deep feral noise that made Lorcan doubt the Asrai's ability.

More swarmed. Jess was covered, almost suffocated.

'They will reduce your amplitude. Foster would say, it is the science of the universe.'

At the mention of his name, Jess snapped her head up. Her eyes were fire and her fingers started to burn.

'The Asrai will burn because of you,' she hissed at him, 'They all burn because of you.'

The air around Jess swayed as it heated up and the screams of the Asrai tortured Lorcan as they fell from Jess like peeling flesh.

'You are the only one who can kill me,' she taunted him, 'But you won't. You can't kill me, without hating yourself.'

Jess stood tall now, her features clear through the flames that engulfed her.

The heat licked at Lorcan's face.

'I will walk through Daron and burn anything that's left. Anyone who stands in my way will be another death for you, Lorcan.' She waited, but no response came. 'And still, you stand there?'

Jess took a deep, rasping breath and dragged her feet to move closer to Lorcan.

'And then, I will walk back into Blair. I might burn that

precious cottage to the ground.'

Lorcan could feel his skin blistering. All around him carnage reigned as Fae fought being swept up in Jess's watery demolition. His body heaved with the weight of the task. She was near him now. The intensity of her fading power was still enough to sear him. His skin started to weep blood.

'I wonder if Foster is still there,' spat Jess, not even flinching at the sound of his name, 'Poor, besotted Foster. He couldn't kill me either. I could watch him burn all over again.'

As the final words came out of her mouth, Lorcan sliced his knife through her chest. He pushed deeper, making bigger cuts, never taking his eyes from hers as she slumped down.

'Forgive me, Jess,' he whispered, 'I wish there was another way.'

Jess felt his hand close around her heart, the pressure was warm. She felt safe. But she also remembered. Everything she had done since she came back, and, everything she would do. She saw it all with no linear order. Destruction. Death. Unstoppable sorrow.

'Tell Foster,' she struggled to speak,'That I forgave you. Tell him that, Lorcan. Because, I do. I forgive you.'

Lorcan bent his forehead to Jess's and held his breath. His chest was lead.

'And tell him he'll always be mine. Nothing can consume that. Nothing can take that away. Tell him … tell him to look for me first, in the next life.'

Lorcan ripped out Jess's heart and squeezed it in his hand until her blood ran down his arms, mixed with his own.

Then with Jess in his lap, he cradled her gently and wept.

*

As the water began to recede and the sky became an exhausted powder blue, silence fell. It was impossible for Lilliana to see the mud soaked bodies, less count them. She stood on her balcony, high above the devastated land, and called towards the lake with her hands. Tiny diamond beads of water danced through her fingers as she whispered her quiet thanks to the Asrai. They had sacrificed themselves for her. They had come when she called, she hadn't had to beg. They had come because they wanted to help.

Lilli didn't know why the Asrai had come at her call, but as she looked down now to where her brother was heaped on the ground wrapping Jess's body with his own she felt a bloom of hope.

Hope, because Lorcan had put the needs of the Fae above everything else. Above Ava.

And, because, for the first time since she became leader... she actually felt like one.

Chapter 19

'Has there been any news of Foster, or Brennan?'

Daron had been carefully sifting through the devastation while Autumn turned to Winter. The sky still kept its distance, mourning in pale grey against the growing whiteness of the mountain caps. Sometimes the beauty of a peach sunset would dilute the concentrated loss of loved ones, only for them to remember seconds later that they were never coming back. Some of the villagers believed the lake had punished them for taking too much magic from its water.

'No,' replied Ava, letting Lilliana's eyes scan the scratches on her face and arms. She pushed a piece of escaping hair back into her hastily constructed bun. 'At least not yet,' she added, wanting to sound hopeful.

'I hope you have been making yourself useful, sister,' remarked Lorcan, entering the dining room. He threw himself into a chair upholstered with cream velvet.

Lilliana moved gracefully across the room and seated herself opposite him. She slowly arranged her green organza skirts as she sat. Lorcan tutted.

'Yes, I have,' she retorted, noting the derision in his voice, and the mud on his boots. 'Just because you two feel the need to get dirty, doesn't mean I'm not doing my bit. This is my kingdom, after all.'

Lorcan raised an eyebrow.

'What about the pass? The Oak,' Lilliana asked, trying not to sound hopeful, 'Do you believe Fae will pass through to the other side ever again?' She thought about Brennan, wondering if that's where he was. 'After all,' she added dryly, 'Ava will surely want to go home? If for nothing else, to change those dreadful clothes!'

Ava couldn't stop herself smiling. It gave her comfort that some things might never change. And whilst Lilliana still insulted Ava at every opportunity, there was a softer, less spiteful tone since Jess had been defeated.

'The villagers gave me these,' replied Ava, 'They were more practical for clearing and building.'

Ava hadn't felt homesick for Blair at all these last few weeks. She had relished helping the villagers alongside Lorcan. They had started calling her Daughter of Heath, and, day by day she felt herself become accepted and acknowledged as one of them. It lessened the numbness of losing Jess all over again.

'It looks quite hopeless at the moment,' interrupted Lorcan, dragging his eyes away from Ava's shape in the fitted top. 'There are particular plants and herbs which might, with the right incantation, undo Jess's work. But, at the moment it's sealed to us, and to any Fae trying to return.' Lorcan had noticed Ava's eyes drop when he mentioned Jess. 'But we simply do not have access to those resources at the moment. Everything is buried, or washed away. And it's not a priority,' he added, 'We need to stay focussed on finding life, or at least finding and honouring our dead.'

'And, that's where I come in, dear brother,' Lilliana leaned forward, ready to reveal what she had been working on. Her yellow eyes sparkled.

Lorcan fidgeted in his chair, slightly annoyed that his sister didn't care that Ava had lost Jess, again, but deciding to say nothing. At least it appeared Lilli was taking her duty seriously and, after all, it was her that called the Asrai to help.

'While it is very noble of you,' she shot a look at Ava, 'Of you both... to be down there, getting... involved. We need something more. We need help. We need to remember we are Fae.' She took a deep breath, 'I've been busy meeting with the Elders every day, and the Elders of our neighbouring realms. They are grateful that Jess was defeated. They know had she not been defeated here, she would have carried on. Who knows what damage she left in the Strangers world, and where she would have gone next, when she had finished with us.' Lilliana was on a roll. She didn't stop at the mention of Jess's name. There was no use pretending. Time to move forward. 'So, they will help us. They will supply the flowers, herbs, incantations, whatever we need. They will give us the means to clear and rebuild with more speed. To aid growth and at least be able to enter the festival of Samhain and honour those who fell in Daron.'

'And what is their price for this?' Lorcan, was impressed, but he didn't trust any of the Elders.

'We have already paid the price,' shot back Lilliana. 'I've told you already. More of our people died than theirs, and they know if Jess had not been stopped, she would have come for their lands and their loved ones next. There will be no further price to pay.'

Lorcan's eyebrow raised again. He was torn between doubting the motives of the Elders, and knowing Daron was desperate for help. He stared at Lilliana, remembering a girl who used to spend the day having her hair plaited.

'But, I have one request.' Lilliana stood now.

'The steps. The Oak. The passage to Blair. I want it all cleared. Whatever incantation or spell. Nobody gives up. We open the gateway.'

Ava looked from Lorcan to Lilliana.

Lilliana's face gave nothing away.

'I'm surprised that's your priority,' Ava commented. It struck her as odd as Lilliana had never shown any interest in Blair.

'Why would you be surprised?' threw back Lilliana, trying to push away thoughts of Brennan, and cover her distress, 'I wouldn't want any Fae from Daron to be trapped in your awful world. I can't imagine how basic and feral it is. And, I wouldn't want to keep you here any longer than we have to.'

'Charming,' replied Ava, determined not to care. 'Do we also need to find a way to thank the Asrai properly?'

Lilliana swung round to face Ava. The word *'we'* irritated her. Lorcan shifted in his chair and stood up.

'Yes,' said Lilliana, looking at her brother carefully, 'I suppose we do. After all, they were a huge help.'

'Huge help?' Ava stared at Lilliana, 'They stopped all this. They took her power. They defeated her.' Ava was astonished at Lilliana's attitude. It was unbearable to say Jess's name and remember that she was gone, it ripped at her throat, but they were all indebted to the Asrai.

Ava saw Lilliana staring at Lorcan.

'That's right isn't it?' she asked Lorcan, 'That's what the

villagers are saying.'

Lilliana waited, wondering what Lorcan was going to say. She had watched her brother rip Jess's heart out. Watched him squeeze it dry. Yes, they owed much to the Asrai, but it was Lorcan, and only Lorcan, that had taken Jess's life.

'Yes,' lied Lorcan. He stared resolutely into Ava's eyes and felt his own blacken, 'We owe so much to the Asrai.'

*

Cedric walked towards Annie's cottage deep in thought. He wondered what would be left of it when he got there. He still thought of it as Annie's, but his eyes filled with sorrow when he thought about the events of the last year. He kept looking ahead, taking in the trail of devastation across Blair, devastation that he now had to retrace. The archway was gone. They had watched it implode. Like a contained explosion, it had boomed angry with power. He thought about the Fae that had managed to get through before Jess destroyed it. He remembered the terror on their faces. Some desperate to usher loved ones to safety, and others … herded in the group and screaming to go back to where loved ones were left behind. Hands outreached in despair, pushing in both directions. Cedric stopped walking to compose himself. His breath was deep, as if he needed to purge his lungs and renew. A shiver of gloom stole through him, reminding him he needed to keep moving. He hadn't found Brennan yet, or Foster. Or Ava. 'Ava,' he murmured her name out loud. He was sure she had been in Daron. More misery rushed down his back. He looked around. Trees lay split and strewn like twigs. The eyes of the forest had retreated so far in, Cedric could hardly sense them. He knew the locals would talk about this as a freak storm. Survey the tiles thrown from their roofs, and the broken fences, tut at the expense and the unpredictability of the weather.

Most of them would anyway.

His mind wandered to Toni and he wished he'd paid more attention to her in the last few weeks. He'd watched her helping the Fae that had come through, and he had watched villagers help. Volunteers from the old quarter of the village she'd said. 'I've been trying to tell you Cedric,' she'd repeated, before being pulled away to tend to another injury. 'There are far more Fae living in Blair than we realised. They live in peace with Strangers. And now, they mourn the loss of Heath more than those left in Daron.'

The cry of a wolf startled Cedric back to where he stood. He was nearly there. His attention was pulled to one lone tree that stood tall with carnage all around it. Quite near the cottage but definitely still in the destructive path Jess would have taken. Some of the earth around it looked freshly turned. It was strange that it hadn't been ripped like the others, but then nothing was strange really, thought Cedric, and he pushed his mind back to finding Foster. He trod carefully around the gorged ground, new bare earth exposed and raw. The sky was clear here, almost white, like a new beginning. The universe had cleansed, the storm had passed.

The cottage still stood. But at least ten rows of pine trees lay fractured around the entire area. Like a giant had walked the perimeter, surveyed the cottage, and then walked off towards the clearing, barging a way through rough grass. It would have been that easy, lamented Cedric.

'Hello?' he called quietly, 'Anyone here?' He could sense someone. He'd felt it for several minutes. He'd wondered if he was being followed, and then decided he was a foolish old man. 'I know someone is here,' he called again, 'I feel you. You need help.' He no longer cared if his words sounded strange, this was not the time to worry about fitting in.

And then, walking to the bedroom, Cedric saw him...

Huddled in the corner, skin blistered, eyes devoid of any hope.

Cedric lowered himself down to the floor, 'Foster.'

*

Ava smiled as she helped the villagers in Daron prepare for the festival of Samhain. Lilliana had sent soldiers to spread the word that this festival would be the biggest Daron had ever seen, lasting four days, and nights. Bonfires would be lit across the meadows to cleanse the ground and encourage new growth. Tables were to be set along the banks of the lake, covered with food and drink for all to share. And there was to be dancing. Music and dancing to honour those who had not survived Jess. Ava thought of her each day, and she thought of Foster. Had Jess killed him? Would she ever see him again?

'What are you thinking about?'

The question pulled Ava back to the group of children crafting disguises and costumes from silks and ribbons.

'I'm wondering if I shall ever see my brother again,' replied Ava honestly. She had no need to hide anything when she was with the villagers. It was so peaceful and easy, compared to being in the castle.

'Ofcourse you will,' came an earnest reply from a little boy with eyes so blue, they could have been made from the middle of the lake.

'And why are you so sure?' Ava bent down and stroked the boy's arm lightly.

'We were taught that during Samhain the boundary between us and the other world could more easily be crossed. If Strangers could find it, they could come into our world.'

'My brother is Foster, son of Heath. He could cross anyway. He is no more a Stranger than I am. I think he might have got stuck on the other side. When the gateway collapsed.'

Ava smiled, as she realised how easily she spoke of Strangers, and Fae, and Heath. As if she'd always known of Fae. As if this was all totally normal.

'Good then, that the festival is four days. Plenty of time for him to break through.'

Unless he's dead, thought Ava. She sighed heavily and fiddled with some heavy velvet being used to fashion a cloak.

'Do you think he is dead?' questioned the little girl that had been listening quietly while she wound ivy into a mask of knitted ribbons.

Ava looked up startled. 'It's a possibility,' she said sadly. These children had all lost someone, so there was no point lying.

'I will leave wine and cake outside for him,' continued the little girl undaunted, 'The Elders taught us that souls of the dead visit our homes during the festival looking to bless us. They bring good spirits to bless our animals to make sure we all make it through the Winter. We always set places at our tables for those we have lost.'

'That's what we are,' shouted three of the other children, now pulling on their finished masks and cloaks and running around each other excitedly. 'We could be dead. We could be alive. We could be spirits.' They giggled as they ran round and round; some of the smaller ones falling over with dizzy enjoyment. 'When we knock at your door, you will never know which.'

The children were soon chanting the words at Ava in frenzied delight, running around her until she couldn't help smiling at their high spirits.

'Ava'

The sound of Lorcan's voice startled the children into silence.

'Hello Lorcan,' said Ava carefully. His forehead was furrowed and his eyes dark, but Ava was learning that was no indication of his mood. He just looked that way most of the time. She tried not to smile at her observation. He wouldn't find her funny.

'When you've finished your game, can I talk to you?' His voice was commanding, but gentler this time. Ava wondered if he was desperate to break free of who he was, and have some fun.

'Want to join in?' she teased. 'We've room for another in the circle.'

There it was. The raised eyebrow.

'Perhaps another time,' he replied with no trace of humour. There are far more important duties for these children to be attending to.' Ava was about to protest, but then he winked at the staring children and held out the cloth bag in his hand. 'Who would like to feed a wolf?' he asked, throwing the bag to the youngest child in the group and moving aside.

'I have something for you too,' he said, ignoring the wide eyed look on Ava's face.

'Well aren't you just full of gifts today.'

'Yes. I am,' he replied seriously. 'And if Foster were here, no doubt he would add that I am indeed full of something other than gifts.'

Spontaneous laughter erupted from Ava. And, as if the muscle movement itself was contagious, she smiled. Her mouth open and free. The more she laughed, the wider her grin became. Ava couldn't remember the last time she had felt this light.

Lorcan stared. The corners of his mouth bent up in a cautious joy watching her.

'It's actually from Lilli.' he said, holding out the parcel under his arm. 'Because she does not wish you to wear work clothes during the festival of Samhain.'

Ava sat cross legged on the ground and stared at the package.

'Should I open it now?'

'Yes. I would like to see if you approve of my sister's choice.'

Ava was intrigued. She carefully pulled on the black silk ribbon holding the delicate gold papers together.

Folded carefully inside was a mass of pure white gauze, which lifted with the breeze as Ava shook it gently. Such beautiful, thin layers of fabric. The finest silver woven in flowers throughout seemed to float with the movement of the skirt. It was breathtaking and uncomplicated, and, as Ava held it against herself she knew the fit would be perfect. She also knew, with no doubt, that Lilliana would not have chosen her such a simple, exquisite gown.

'Thank you.' She turned to face Lorcan, but he had already walked away, to join his wolves.

*

Cedric didn't speak, he just sat in silence with his hands wrapped around Fosters. The room smelt of fire. Cedric could see furniture upturned, and linens smouldering, but the damage was minimal. At least, he pondered, looking at Foster, the damage was minimal to the things that could be replaced.

When Foster finally spoke, it was to no one in particular. He didn't look at Cedric; He didn't look at anything. His focus was nowhere, and everywhere, searching out for answers that would never come.

'Can you imagine?' he said quietly, 'What it's like to know you are weak? You know what you have to do. And it grips at every nerve. That you have to kill the one person you love, rather than live with what they have become. What you created. You tell yourself that the price you'll pay is worth it, because you will have saved so many. But when it comes to it, when you look into their eyes and see the shadow of who they were, screaming at you to help them. Could you do it? Does it make you the monster too?'

Cedric didn't answer. He knew Foster wasn't expecting one. And he did know. He felt the grip of regret and self loathing that he had walked away from Kallan and Heath so many years ago. He created men of majesty and destruction, and deserted them when he could no longer live with the consequences.

'And then I realised,' Foster looked at Cedric now, but it was impossible to know if he saw the old man, 'I love her. She had become violent, chaotic, unstoppable. I knew she had killed. I knew she would kill more. So many more. But I realised that wasn't enough for me.' He paused, closing his eyes against the horror of his own words. 'Even that. That wasn't enough for me to stop her.' Tears started to clean a line down Foster's emotionless face. The only clue to the fermenting chaos inside. 'I realised I would rather die than live without either version of her.' He spoke slowly at the end, as if he couldn't quite believe it himself.

'Foster, I am going to get help,' Cedric spoke now, calmly, and with a kindness that radiated out to the creatures brave enough to venture from their hiding places. 'At the very least I shall find water to heal your burns.'

'I want to keep the burns,' muttered Foster, 'I want to keep the last thing she gave me. I want to feel the blistering heat of her touch.' He looked at his bloodied hands. 'I tried to push the knife through us both. I tried to end us together.' He opened his shirt to reveal a long wound, ragged and oozing, but held together with what looked to Cedric like powdery ice.

'Stay here,' replied Cedric, sensing Foster had no urge to leave, 'I will not be long.'

Foster felt Cedric leave. He knew the warmth had left the room.

'So many dead,' he said to no one. 'So many dead because I wanted her back. At any cost.'

He heard footsteps, but he wasn't afraid.

'I brought her back, and she destroyed families.'

He wondered if wolves were waiting at the door, but he didn't care enough to investigate.

'I tried to slice her throat while she conspired with the universe. I watched as the last fragment of Jess pushed through to seek me out. I saw her sorrow, and I saw the strain of holding on. I watched her come undone, disintegrate in front of me, the last thread of Jess healed me, while the chaos consumed her.'

He closed his eyes, sensing someone in the room, but not

caring if he lived or died.

'I loved her, still,' he whispered defiantly, 'I loved every version of her. And I'm done with the universe. I will never care about anyone again. I, am done.'

Tabby waited until she was sure Foster was unconscious. When he hadn't moved for several minutes, she tip toed across the room to where he slumped. Pulling a ragged crochet blanket from the bed she curled up on the floor next to him placing her head in his lap. She had lost everyone she loved too. She had crawled her way out with bloodied hands and feet before the passage from Daron to Blair had shattered against her back. Now, this man was saying it was his fault. She didn't know if she believed him. But for now, they could keep each other company. Keep each other warm, until help came.

Chapter 20

Lilliana stood on the balcony of the Great Hall and watched the dancing below. It had been this way her whole life. Always observing. She couldn't remember a time when she had closed her eyes and abandoned herself to the throbbing rhythm of the music. She longed to lose herself in the sea of colour. She wondered what it would be like, just for a moment, to be someone else. But the thought didn't last. She was exactly where she wanted to be. She was exactly where she had told everyone she would be one day. The Elders might be muttering amongst themselves, but here she was - despite them. A woman. In charge. She looked down at them now; they were all watching, waiting. She placed her hands on her hips, feeling the tightness of the black leather corset. Under the vivid layers of organza she wore leather leggings. It was easier to keep knives strapped securely that way. And it was easier to run. Lilli flinched as Brennan flickered across her mind. He was always there, she realised now, but some thoughts pinched at her more than others. He had taught her to wear the weapons. He had advised her seamstress on making beautiful clothes that wouldn't restrict her should she need to fight. Where was he? Did he go to Blair? Was he trapped there? Was he alive? She closed her eyes at the last thought. The idea that he might never come back scorched her chest. Anguish flooded her. She stretched her fingers out in annoyance. She needed to be stronger, she chastised herself. A mist of water swirled at her feet, reminding her it was time to talk to the crowd gathered below.

*

Ava watched Lorcan dancing. He moved with confidence, but she sensed he wasn't completely comfortable as he made courteous conversation with Fae that she guessed were influential to Daron. He politely danced amongst gowns so vibrant and fluid, Ava imagined him to be swimming in a shoal of tropical fish.

But his eyes, were on her.

The way his eyes had always been on her.

She stared back.

She saw him wince with pain from wounds that still needed time. She saw rage and obsession. Closing her eyes she allowed herself to wallow in the thought of him. She breathed deeply, know the intensity of his darkness was fusing into longing, a thirst to be near her. When she first met Lorcan, all she'd seen in those eyes was the deep, inky poison. A reason to run. Now, she opened her eyes watching him move through the crowd towards her. She held his stare, and allowed a bliss to soak through her.

*

Lilliana was ready. She stepped forward and held her hand up to the crowd below. The water running through the walls fizzed and filled the room with a mist that quietened the music and ended the dancing. It floated towards the balcony and shrouded Lilli. When she emerged through to face her people, the mist beaded and framed in perfect pearls.

She scanned the crowd for Brennan. And then took a deep breath.

'I am young,' she began honestly, and determined not to be undermined. 'But I am learning.' She raised her voice a little more. 'I am learning a leader is wise. She earns her serenity, and her value. Time must, and will, test her. She will not have admiration simply bestowed on her, as a right of birth.' Lilli knew the Elders were listening closely. But she had chosen these words with Brennan's caution and balance running through her soul. She would not allow the Elders to destabilise her. She would not be weak. 'I will suffer, and I will grow more beautiful each day because of our suffering. I will become your vision.' Her voice was strong and she noticed the Fae below leaning closer, paying attention – looking hopeful. 'I care deeply for the people of Daron. I am with you, and I will remember that being your leader is an honour. An honour that is bigger than me. I will serve you. And, I will hold this kingdom together. I will not wait for our destiny, as if it is a matter of chance. I will achieve a destiny of our choosing.'

Lilli heard clapping. It started faintly, perhaps one Fae at a time, but it was building momentum, fusing with water as it bounced towards her.

'I know I am young,' she repeated, at a volume she had never felt running from her body, 'But I am no longer foolish. I ask you to believe in me. I ask you to embrace me as your leader. We will rebuild Daron. We will rebuild, and we will prosper. And, I promise you, we will find meaning in our loss. The Fae *will* live on forever.'

*

'The gown suits you,' said Lorcan carefully. Ava thought his eyes would burn the fabric away.

'Thank you,' she replied staring straight at him, 'Who knew your sister would be so generous, and flatter me so well.' The statement was loaded, she made no pretence otherwise.

Lorcan continued to stare, saying nothing, until Ava moved her eyes to the pieces of thick black silk wound tightly around his arm. She'd noticed other people with ribbons too.

'It's for Tha gaol. A dance of the Fae,' he added when he saw Ava's eyebrows lift in confusion.

'You haven't danced with me yet,' she added matter of factly. The music had slowed, but was vibrant and pulsing. Ava noticed some of the Fae unwinding the ribbons from each other.

'This dance is about passion.' He felt his heart quicken as Ava's fingers pulled at the knotted ribbon on his arm. 'The vital life force that moves within and amongst us.' Ava started to unwind the ribbon from his arm, wrapping it over and over her own hand. 'To dance this with me, is to bind us together. Our bodies will be connected by this silk.'

Ava pulled at the ribbon.

'Ava, this is a dance for lovers.'

Lorcan could hardly breathe as Ava's mouth came up to his ear. He felt her breath against his skin.

'Then dance it with me, Lorcan.'

'Very eloquent.'

Lilliana pulled her gaze away from the swarm of colour below her, and turned around.

'I meant every word,' she replied carefully, keeping her voice steady and serious.

The Elders standing in front of her didn't reply. Their robes were heavy and sober. Ornate, but pompous.

'What can I do for you?' she asked, feeling alone, the euphoria of her speech slipping away.

'As you instructed,' replied an Elder, lowering his hood and bowing his head to Lilliana, 'The flowers and herbs needed to speed the recovery of Daron have arrived. The incantation will be delivered to the pass at dawn tomorrow, along with further supplies. Quite a quantity. Enough to open the gateway to the other side.'

Lilliana's stomach skipped. She was sure Brennan was there. Every search party she had sent out within Daron had come back with no sighting.

She took a deep breath, 'Good,' she replied unsmiling.

'We do, however, need you to follow us.' The Elder speaking started to turn away.

'Follow you? Why? I will decide when it is time to leave.'

The Elder stopped abruptly, and turned around.

'Because, Your Majesty, you need to agree the price.'

*

It didn't matter to Lorcan that Ava had never seen the dance before. The room fell away from him, just as it had the last time they danced together. The music pulsed through his body as he gripped the end of the ribbons and pulled her to him. Ava's wrists lurched forward. Grabbing at Lorcan's shoulders she pushed her body against him, willing him to hold her. He responded, wrapping the end of the silks around his own hands until their fingers touched. Ava let the heat slide down her body. She trembled as he pushed her arms up above her head, gripping her fingers through his own. His lips traced her neck.

'The ribbons fuse us, throughout the dance. Do not let go of the ribbon.'

Ava heard the words against her neck. He brought her arms down and unwound the ribbons enough to trail his fingers down her body resting on her hips.

'If you feel our bodies move apart, use the ribbons,' he whispered against her cheek. His lips so close to hers she dug her fingers into his skin rather than give in to the temptation to kiss him.

As the music grew louder, Ava pushed her hands through Lorcan's hair. She pressed herself against him, and pulled at the ribbon, willing him to touch her. The colours of the room were a blur and a fine mist shielded them from prying eyes as their bodies moved.

Lorcan wound the ribbons tight once again, pulling Ava's hands up to his face. She touched him gently at first, tracing the line of the scar across his chin. And then his fingers moved down grazing her throat and collarbone. Ava stared at him. She could feel his heart beat. And then his mouth covered hers. His breath warm inside her. As his lips gently pulled at hers she pressed against him, opening her mouth to deepen the kiss.

And then he stopped. He stopped moving completely, but their bodies were still locked together. Ava pressed her forehead against Lorcan's chin, still feeling the pressure on her mouth where his had been.

'Do you still deny you want me?' Her voice was softly challenging, and she felt breathless.

'Look at me,' he requested.

Ava tilted her head up ready to argue with any excuse he came up with.

Lorcan's lips hovered over hers, no space between them. 'Want you?' he replied, his eyes haunted, 'I don't just want you. I love you.'

Ava wanted to smile, but she knew he wasn't finished. She had that now familiar feeling that nothing with Lorcan was ever uncomplicated.

'I have tried to deny it. To you, but mostly to myself. I believed I could refuse my own doomed feelings. Force myself to discredit them.'

Ava wondered if she should be offended. It certainly sounded offensive. 'Wait, so...'

'Let me finish,' he continued, 'I may never have the courage to say this again, and we have a habit of misunderstanding each other.'

Ava pulled back slightly from Lorcan, and she saw his eyes flinch. She held tight to the ribbons, tugged at them gently, and stayed quiet.

'The more I denied my feelings, the stronger they grew. With each effort to act within the rules of my upbringing and ancestry, I determined every action, regardless of consequence. Each time, I found myself falling further in love and further away from everything I know.'

Ava took his hands and held them to her face. She kissed them gently, and then rested them against her heart. Their faces pressed against one another.

'When Sorcha was returned to us,' he whispered, 'My heart ripped in that second that I thought it was you. And then afterwards, when I should have been rejoicing that you were safe, I felt shame. For a fleeting second I realised I loved you so much, that it would have been easier if you had died. It would have meant moving on, living with boiling regret and loss. But easier in my arrogance, than having to accept, as I did in that moment, that I would always love you. That you, Ava, could have all of me. If you had died, then I wouldn't have the choice. I wouldn't have to live with the regret of pushing you away. Wouldn't have to live with knowing I walked away.'

The music hadn't stopped. Couples still swam around them, lost in the passion of their dance.

Lorcan looked into Ava's eyes. Searching for her response. Wondering if he'd said enough, or too much. Instantly regretting saying all of it.

Ava unwound just one silk ribbon from their wrists.

And then, weaving her fingers with his, she led Lorcan by the hand out of the Great Hall.

*

'What do you mean, agree the price?'

Lilliana strode off the balcony following the Elders. Her voice losing its former composure as her strides became quicker.

'I am not sure we understand your question, Your Majesty. The help from the other realms is not without a price.'

'But we have already paid a price. You can see that. Did you not tell them that?'

'The quantity of materials required to open a sealed gateway is vast. And some of the leaves and petals required are from the most endangered plants, in the most inaccessible, remote parts of our planet.'

'Yes, I know that. But we defeated the creature that used to be Stranger. You see the damage she has done to Daron. She would have carried on. She would have caused havoc across the realms.'

'The incantation is ancient.'

'I know that too.' Lilliana's voice was rising. She clenched her fists and resisted the urge to scream at the Elders. Why had she thought they would accept a woman as their leader?

'You wanted the passage to Blair cleared. You wanted the gateway open. That is not an easy task.'

'I am getting very tired of the sound of your voice,' shouted Lilliana. 'What have you done? What have you agreed to without my authority?'

'We have agreed a fair price. One that will ensure the other realms have a reason to help us, a reason for future solidarity, and harmony across many Fae realms.'

Lilliana felt the words like a blow to her stomach. They lurched over and she felt an odd mixture of anger and nausea.

'A price that will help you fulfil your promise that Daron will endure and rise again.'

Lilliana wanted to sink to her knees. She knew what was coming. She knew without a doubt what the Elders had promised behind her back. Her head was spinning, but she refused to collapse in front of them. She needed to get away. She picked up her skirt and turned her back on the men silently watching her.

As she ran, only one word swirled around her head, picking up speed and mutating until it drowned out any other thought. A thousand versions of the same word, spinning and mocking her.

Marriage.

*

It was Ava that led Lorcan to his own room, and opened the heavy wooden door pulling him inside. But it was Lorcan that pushed the door shut, pressing her against the wall with such purpose her feet left the ground.

As he held her face and kissed her mouth, she heard the words again,

'I don't just want you. I love you.'

Her stomach tightened as his mouth moved slowly down to her throat. She arched her back as his teeth grazed her skin.

When she pulled at the top covering his bandages, he winced, but the sound he made against her skin was dangerous and untamed.

'You said I could have all of you.' Her words were quiet against his ear, and he wrapped his arms around her pressing his body against hers.

'Is that what you want?' His voice was vulnerable, his breathing heavy.

Ava ran her hand down his chest, lingering on the tight muscles across his stomach. She closed her eyes and let his fingers slowly unfasten each clasp of her dress.

'What I want is to forget, just for tonight, all of the reasons why this cannot work.'

He laid her down in the cushions and pressed their bodies together. Intoxicating desire crushed any space between them.

'I want to stay with you. I want you to love me,' she murmured against his warm skin, 'I want to be the one that soothes the darkness in your soul.'

*

Lilliana stood firm at the bottom of the steps leading to the Great Oak. There was a time when she would have frowned at moss stains and wet earth, complained loudly at having to be here, so near the gateway to Blair. But, that was then. That was a time when she believed she could be anything she wanted to be. That was when she thought she could change the kingdom. Rid it of its antiquated, outdated traditions and rules. As the words from an ancient language were read from a scroll as delicate as tissue, a fire raged at the mouth of the gateway. Aromas from burning coral tree and underground orchid were suffocating. Lilliana took a step closer, not caring that her face would dirty or her boots scorch.

Finally one of the Elders turned to her.

'It is done. When the fire dies, the gateway will be open. The Oak will smoulder for days to come, but with disintegration will come transformation.'

'Good. Then leave me now,' said Lilliana curtly. She met the stare of the Elder firmly.

'I believe it would be appropriate for you to come back with us. There are soldiers that can wait at the entrance.'

'Do you think I care about what is appropriate?' Lilliana's voice was calm, but edged with anger.

'I insist, Your Majesty.'

'I said, leave.'

'I don't think you quite understand how you should behave.'

'And I don't think you quite understand who is in charge here.' Lilliana's voice rose with each word. Her glare was ice.

'It would be unwise to follow your own direction,' the Elder would not be silenced. 'You must amend and repent for allowing the half-Fae to roam our realms buying freedom for women bought fairly at the souks. The other realms will not forget and demand the price be paid. I will send for soldiers, to accompany you back.'

'You,' roared Lilliana, now raising a hand towards the Elder and curling her fingers to caress and shape the beads of water spiralling around her wrists, 'You will leave. I will not be your puppet. Leave, or I will strike you down. All of you.'

Before the Elder had a chance to reply, Lilliana pulled her hand back and shot not only needle shards of water at the hooded man, but a six inch blade of sharpened silver.

*

Anyone who knew Lorcan and Lilliana as they grew up, would have stared in disbelief at them as sunrise took hold and gently flooded Daron with a rose glow.

Proud, arrogant Lorcan, with an inescapable duty to rule the Fae of Daron, was entwined with Ava. The impossible half Fae who argued and challenged every belief he had ever held. As their naked bodies held each other tightly and he kissed her deeply, Lorcan let go of the last shreds of belief, that he could survive without her.

And Lilliana. The pampered, indulged child with aspirations to rule and change Daron, was now fighting for the right to choose her future. She was no stranger to fierce, but this was new, feral. She climbed the steps, towards the middle of the Great Oak, alone. She hated the other side. She hated the Strangers. And she felt fear for the first time. She took one last look down at the Elders strewn across the foot of the steps. This wasn't a tantrum, this was real. No one would choose for her. No one would tell her who or when she should marry.

The wolves that had gathered at the foot of the steps howled. Lilliana stumbled at the sound.

'You better be there, Brennan,' she said out loud, taking a

deep breath to steady herself, before disappearing through the smouldering Oak and leaving Daron.

Chapter 21

'People in town are saying that Heath isn't coming back. That he was killed on the other side.'

Tabby set the food down in Annie's cottage, and sat down next to Foster.

'Why do you keep coming back here?' asked Foster, picking up the sandwich and taking a hungry mouthful.

'They are saying it was the blonde man that killed him. But I met him, and he seemed nice.'

'Not everyone is what they appear to be, Tabby.'

'When you're ready, will you come with me and meet the others? They won't mind that you loved Jess. They will understand.'

It had been the same each day. Tabby would bring food to Foster, and talk about the families that were looking after her. She talked of how they had all grown closer and made a pact that they would survive even without Heath. Foster had taken no notice to start with. He was so wrapped up in his own private torment that he'd listened without hearing. He wasn't even sure how many times Tabby had come. He slept on Annie's bed in between her visits and thought about Tabby losing everyone she loved. She talked about it all the time, but she didn't cry in front of him. He realised that was for his benefit, she was trying to reach out and heal his pain. He felt shame.

'How can it be that so many on this side, in Blair I mean, how can it be that so many knew Heath?'

Foster took another bite of sandwich and Tabby smiled pushing the bag closer to him. She liked that he finally wanted to talk.

'I've been trying to tell you. There's lots of us. Lots of rainbow families.'

'Here! In Blair you mean?'

'Yes.' Tabby smiled. It seemed simple to her. It amazed her that it should be any other way, and she thought of the times her parents had reminded her to talk less.

'I am Fae, but my little brother, Raz, is half Fae.' She frowned at the thought of Raz and felt the familiar burning in her throat. She hadn't found him yet. It suffocated her words. But she took a gulp of air and blinked hard. 'My Daddy isn't, wasn't, Fae, but he loved me.'

'And he was - well?' Foster wondered how much the little girl would understand.

Tabby looked confused, and then exclaimed, 'Oh, you mean that stuff about using him up?'

Foster smiled. It was the kindest thing he had heard in some time. 'I think that's what I mean,' he replied.

'Daddy told me that he was enchanted by how beautiful me and mummy were. He said that no love could match how he loved us, as the Fae were very special. He said it was using him up more quickly than other daddies. Mummy said she couldn't help loving him, and she would do anything to keep him.'

'Sounds quite a love story.' Foster was intrigued to know how many Fae lived like this. 'Bet that doesn't happen very often?'

'Course it does.'

'You're really telling me lots of Fae live here? How many?'

'I don't count them silly. They're just here, and Heath was working on a way to stop the Strangers getting used up.

And a way to keep the Fae safe.'

'What?'

'I don't really understand it, I'll get it wrong if I tell it.'

'Tabby,' Foster was sitting up straighter now, 'Just tell me what you know. Anything.'

'There was a lady that used to live here,' began Tabby. She hesitated, looking around at the cosiness of the room. She decided she would have liked to live here.

'You mean Annie?'

'Yes. Annie.' Tabby smiled at Foster, feeling more confident now she felt he knew who Annie was. 'Heath told us that he loved her. And her love in return made him strong. It filled him with courage and it was enough to keep them both warm and know true happiness.'

Tabby's words enchanted Foster. He had spent so many nights wondering if his father had seduced Annie with the purpose of making a half-Fae to sacrifice. A calculated attempt to remove all Strangers free will and force a return to the devotion of the Fae. Had Heath been as bad as Kallan all along? But now, listening to Tabby his heart felt pinched and twisted for the fate of his parents, and the reminder of his love for Jess.

'But she died,' said Tabby quietly. 'Not of old age, or illness, but from loving a Fae. It was the way it has always been.' She lifted her chin quoting old words she remembered being told over and over when she visited Daron, 'My Gramme said, the love and adoration of the Strangers will make us dazzle. It will keep the lands green and the crops strong. We will be blessed with magic. But to love too deeply will bring heartbreak. You will drain the very last drop of life from that which you love more than life itself. Some thought it was a punishment, for breaking the rules.'

Foster waited. Tabby hadn't really explained anything he didn't already know, but he didn't want to push her. 'I had heard that,' he decided to reply gently, hoping it would prompt her forward.

'Heath decided to change that,' she said, as if changing it was the easiest thing in the world to do. 'He said, that over and over through the ages, the universe was determined to make new beginnings. He said there was no reason for people to get used up so quickly. He had a way to help everyone. A way to keep the Strangers from getting used up too quickly and a way for the Fae to live wherever they wish free from the bad people. He was working on a medicine.'

It all sounded so simple. So ridiculous, and so simple. How was that even possible? But, then Foster reminded himself, everything that had happened over the last year was ridiculous and impossible.

'Want to know a secret, Tabby?'

She looked at him, excited, 'Tell me. I promise to keep it.'

'I am Heath's son.'

Tabby's eyes were wide, 'And was Annie your mummy?'

'Yes,' he said softly. 'But they never saw me grow up. They didn't get to love me.'

Tabby threw her arms around Foster's neck and hugged him hard. For the first time since he had met her, Foster hugged Tabby back.

*

Cedric sat in Maria's café. It was damaged, but not beyond repair. It would be a while before it was open again, but many of Blair's residents were determined it would be back in business to honour Maria, who they assumed had been killed during the terrible storm that ripped through their village.

Toni placed her hand carefully over Cedric's, it was not often she saw him lost for words.

'I am sorry I know so little,' she said quietly, 'It's only now, with Heath gone, that people are talking to me about it. I assume Heath started to work on this after Annie died. Or perhaps before, we will never know.' She paused, contemplating Heath's dread of Annie's inevitable decline, before adding, 'And the alarm and panic that Jess has caused is making it even harder to get information.'

'Do you know what was in this medicine? Or how long the people have been taking it? Do we even know if it worked?'

Toni shook her head.

'I don't know how I missed this,' she replied, 'Everyone kept it from me. I only know this small amount because I've had to treat some of the children who grew sick. Stranger and Fae.'

'Which would suggest Heath's work was not complete?'

'Perhaps. But you and I were unaware of the many Fae living in Blair, and until last year The Order kept their distance. So, Heath may have indeed found a way to disguise their identity.'

'Can you imagine?' Cedric mused, 'Fae and Strangers living as families. Equal, undamaged.'

'And children unhindered by the rules of history.' The sound of Brennan's drawl made Cedric jump from his seat.

'Where did you come from?' he cried, throwing his arms around Brennan with relief, 'I didn't dare hope...' Cedric's voice trailed off as he swallowed the sob that wretched from his chest.

'I am sorry to have caused you distress, old man.' Brennan folded his father in his arms. 'There has been much to do, to help Blair. Fae and Stranger alike.'

'So you know? You have heard there are families living here in Blair? You have heard of the magic Heath created, to hide Fae and keep the Strangers they love from fading?'

'I have seen it with my own eyes now,' replied Brennan. 'It is not perfect. There is work still to do.'

'I am glad you see it that way,' said Cedric, pulling back from Brennan and taking a deep breath.

'Do you not?' And then, before Cedric had a chance to answer Brennan added, 'How many more centuries must we spend fighting? Searching for an adoration that no one can remember. Chasing a truth in scriptures written so long ago, perhaps they are just bed time stories.'

Cedric sighed, feeling his old life haunting him as it always did. Like a shadow. Sometimes in front, sometimes lurking behind. Unable to pull free, always connected to his soul. 'It would be a blessing,' he concluded, 'I would welcome the unity and peace. But just because the solution might exist, does not mean everyone will welcome it. Never forget there are forces on both sides that do not want stability. When they hear of this, they will fight even harder to ensure both sides stay one step away from killing each other. They see no profit in peace.'

'Cedric is right.' The woman's voice caught them all by surprise. Everyone swung round and stared. 'Although I can scarce believe any Fae would want to live here.'

'Your Majesty!' Cedric and Toni spoke at the same time, both stunned for something else to say.

*

'You came to look for me.' Brennan grinned, watching Lilliana walk slowly around Maria's kitchen.

They had been alone for a while, but had the spent the time cautiously making small talk.

'No. I came to look for Cedric, I need his help.' Lilliana felt her cheeks burn at Brennan's teasing.

'Well that's strange, as I could have sworn you said you hated this side, and, you almost threw your arms around me when you walked in earlier.' His grin grew wider knowing that Lilliana would never admit she had come all this way, alone, for him.

Lilliana dragged her hand over the pine table in the middle of the room. 'Do Strangers really make do with such, small, rooms?' she asked, avoiding his stare.

'You are such a spoilt…,' he wanted to say brat, but just in that second, she looked fierce again. Her hair was blazing with red curls that cascaded down her back like rolling fire. 'Actually, this was a café, and the woman who ran it was Fae. She lived with the Strangers for many years, very happily.'

'Hmm,' was all Lilliana said at first. She looked around at the gleaming ovens and shelves piled with baking pans.

'Have you even visited your own kitchens? I know for a fact you have never wandered to the villages along the lake. Never sat at the wooden tables of ordinary Fae and shared their wine.' He was edging closer to her now, and Lilliana smiled wanting him to touch her.

'And why would I want to do that, Brennan?' she asked slowly, knowing she was going to taunt him. 'If I want to spend time with ordinary Fae, I have you.' She challenged him with her eyes as she finished speaking.

Brennan leaned closer to her, fixing her stare, 'So I was right,' he smiled, 'You came to Blair to find me.' He gently picked up the curl covering her cheek and twisted it around his finger. 'You stepped through to the world of Strangers just to find a lowly, ordinary soldier.'

Their faces were nearly touching, and both could feel the small space between them hot against their skin.

'Don't make me do it again, soldier,' she whispered, her breathing heavier as she felt Brennan's arm slip around her waist.

Brennan smiled, and then his mouth covered hers as he drew her close. Lilliana pressed herself against him wrapping her arms around his neck.

As their kiss deepened the air around them slowed.

'I thought I had lost you,' It was a whisper, but Brennan felt the words against his mouth.

'It is my duty to protect you,' he replied, moving his hands across her hips and up her back to where her bodice fastened.

'Is that all it is?' She smiled as she asked, she already knew the answer. She felt his fingers graze down her spine as each button came undone.

'Yes,' he breathed against her neck as he kissed her, 'That is all.' And with one movement she was on the table, her back against the smooth cool wood.

'I don't think this is what the table was intended for. Are there not rules?' She was smiling as she pulled Brennan down on top of her.

His answer was almost inaudible, murmured against her skin.

'And when, exactly, have you ever followed the rules?'

*

'You promised to deliver the weapon to us. Where is she

now?'

Carter stood tall. Three guns, pointed at his head. He could probably knock each of these Strangers to the floor with one movement, but right now he didn't care if he lived or died. He had watched as the gateway reopened, crouched and hidden. He had followed Lilliana to the village green, watched as she joined Cedric, Atonia and then Brennan at the café. So many Fae in the wrong place he smiled, congratulating himself on the plan forming.

Chapter 22

The air chilled Carter as he walked towards Maria's café. Turning up the collar on his long waxy coat he looked at the broken trees and ripped turf around the green. It reminded him how unobservant and short sighted the Strangers were. Intricate root systems clawed upwards, and some trunks embedded so tightly into the earth they looked as if they had been there for years. How could the witless Strangers be happy to accept this was a freak storm? He felt a pang of guilt that he was leading The Order towards Lilliana. The eyes of the forest watched him stride forward. He could feel their stare. But what did he care? He had no one to answer to. He made his own luck.

Carter's boot forced through the locked door with one kick.

'Now this, I did not expect!' he exclaimed, kicking aside some chairs and raising his arms to liberate the knives strapped to his arms. He smiled at the zinging noise they made as he triggered their release.

Brennan sprang to his feet, half dressed, but holding the small sword that had stayed by his side all night. 'I might have known you would survive,' he said slowly, his voice deep with loathing. 'I was right to not trust you.'

'Yes, congratulations,' replied Carter with no humour. He looked at Lilliana sitting up now, clutching blankets against herself. She looked… glowing and content, and then immediately afraid. 'I am sure you will be rewarded for your loyalty, soldier.' He felt an unusual rage towards Brennan, a resentment. 'But, by the looks of it,' he added, looking directly at Lilliana, 'You already have.'

'How. Dare. You,' roared Lilliana.

'Well I think the situation speaks for itself, My Lady,' replied Carter. He made sure to look at Lilliana slowly, lingering on her shoulders, but then immediately regretted the look it cast across her face.

'Enough of this,' shouted one of the men standing behind Carter. 'Who is this girl? Is this the one we have come for? Is this the weapon?'

'Get dressed,' ordered Carter.

'So you're working for them now,' goaded Brennan. 'Do

they know you were planning to double cross them? Do they know you planned to use Jess against them? Or did you plan to hand her over? Who's side are you on?'

'I work for no one,' shouted Carter. And then he lowered his voice and smirked. 'Don't you get it. Why can't you see you are all as bad as each other? I don't care if the Strangers live or die. I don't care if Daron falls and perishes. I hoped you would all kill each other. I wanted to watch you all burn. I wanted to rid this land of every last one of you, and watch a new order rise.'

'And I suppose you thought that would put you in charge?'

Carter raised his head back and laughed. Because it really was that ridiculous to him. 'You are all so stupid.'

Everyone took a step closer to him.

'To be in charge requires a plan. It requires an outcome. It requires me... to care. And most of all it requires me to survive. And that's what made my plan perfect. I didn't care. I don't need to survive. I just need to show you all. I just need to win.'

Lilliana stood in the doorway, now dressed in the bodice and leggings she'd worn into Blair. She gripped the skirt in her hand, knowing this was a time for running.

Carter's eyes sparkled like turquoise sea foam.

'You have completely lost the plot,' she said loudly.

He snapped his gaze to her and for a second his eyes calmed as he took in the ruby curls piled high on her head and the amber of her eyes. She looked defiant.

'There is no plot,' he replied calmly, 'There is only chaos, as we stand still and let time move around us. We change nothing, and nothing changes us.'

'Quite so, Carraeir,' announced Cedric, approaching the men of The Order through the broken café front and flicking his wrist towards the guns they carried. The weapons twisted growing too hot to hold. They clattered to the floor leaving the men to reach urgently for the knives under their jackets.

'Power and greed slice through our worlds like a fever,' said Cedric, looking sadly at Carter, and then to each of them in turn. 'We live in chaos and ingratitude. The Fae are diminished. Their magic now scarce, their fertility precious. And they fight. They fight each other for a time they cannot remember when harmony danced through both worlds. And the Strangers continue to worship false Gods. So many different Gods. They seek violence, utter carnage, in the pursuit of pleasing these Gods. Without once looking at one another to acknowledge they are all lost.'

'Enough waffle.' One of The Order stepped forward towards Lilliana, 'The Fae are demons. To be eradicated by any means necessary.'

'And what then?' Cedric remained calm, stepping between the man and Lilliana, 'The Order succeeded in causing the demotion of Fae to mere folklore. But you know that's not true. You have seen enough to know they exist. Perhaps in a dwindled state, but you see we are hidden in plain sight. Kill one of us, kill all of us here today, but we will not be eradicated. We have existed in secrecy for thousands and thousands of years. You are one man. Many live among you. Everywhere. In peace with both worlds. They work. They marry. They love.'

'And soon they will all die,' said another of The Order. 'Why are we wasting our time here. We just create bodies to hide. Let's leave and let the poison do its job. Why get our hands dirty, when the demon has betrayed his own kind.'

Silence fell. Just for a few seconds. Quiet, still, confusion.

Cedric turned his head slowly to look at Carter.

'Don't look at me, old man,' Carter's voice was steady and serious. 'I don't know what they're talking about.'

'You don't know then?' said the man, his lips twisted somewhere between sly and smug.

'Come on, let's just leave,' said the last of the three men, 'We don't need to explain anything to them, they'll find out soon enough.'

'But don't you want to see their faces?'

'Not really, and what if they come up with a plan to stop us?'

Cedric continued to stare at Carter, 'What have you done?' he asked, his eyes searching out Carter's with a sadness that seemed old and knowing.

'I told you,' replied Carter, his voice strained for the first time, 'I don't know of any poison.' He wondered if he should be afraid, but in truth he was agitated that The Order may have outwitted him.

'Well I do want to see their faces,' smirked the first man, leaning towards Lilliana and picking up the curl that rested on her shoulder.

'Take your hands off her,' warned Brennan.

The man ignored him. 'I want it to be written into the history books that human kind finally defeated the demons. We poisoned every last one of them living in our world, along with any traitor that consorted with them.'

'How is that possible?' Brennan was raising up his knife now. He would cut this man's hand off if he didn't stop touching Lilliana.

'Enough!' shouted the third man, 'Leave the woman. Let's go.'

'Not till I take a piece of her hair.' His face was leering as his finger touched her skin.

Brennan sliced his knife across the man's stomach, the blade so sharp it was like cutting jelly. Blood spat across Lilliana.

Leaning closer to the dying man Brennan hissed, 'What poison? Who is responsible?'

Unlike Carter, Brennan did not believe in chaos. He did not believe we stand still and let time move around us. He believed we change everything, all the time, with every decision. And even the smallest decision can change your life forever…

Sometimes, though, not for the better… He felt the liquid being sprayed as he lent closer to man's mouth. It tasted bitter. He felt it sting his gums and burn the back of his throat as it melted away. He knew as he slumped forward against the bleeding Stranger that poison was snaking through his body, slowly, and he wondered if he had heard the words correctly or if he was dead already.

'Heath,' rasped the man, desperate to cause one last wound, 'Heath despised you all as much as we do.'

Chapter 23

Cedric was at Brennan's side before his head hit the floor.

'No,' he whimpered, 'None of this is right.'

He didn't hear the commotion around him, it all faded to blurred white noise as he mumbled words of sorcery from the ancients across Brennan's twisted face. 'I cannot lose you,' he whispered, his face wet with tears, 'I would die a thousand, pain drenched deaths, rather than lose you now.'

Behind him, Lilliana's hand shot forward, her fingers stretched with anger, 'What have you done?' she screamed at one of the men, 'Tell me what you have given him or I will snap your neck from here.'

The man fell to his knees gripping his throat, his eyes already starting to bulge.

Next to him, the third guard from The Order was silent. His hands up in submission as Carter held two knives crossed against his neck.

'You heard her. Speak.'

'We have been listening. Finally, listening. Learning about our enemy,' gasped the man staring at Lilliana, desperately trying to get breath in, 'We studied your ways. We took what we wanted from the best parts of you.'

Lilliana twisted her wrist around and Carter could see his windpipe moving under his skin.

'Let him speak,' he shouted at her, but he moved the blades against his prisoner's skin for good measure watching the small line of blood form against them.

'You have to die,' he whispered, 'All of you. How can we live with people that think they can control us. You would strike a man dead for choosing the wrong god. No one person should have that much power.'

No one person except you, thought Carter, and he took a deep breath against the urge to end the life in front of him.

'It is the venom of the cone snail,' muttered Cedric, his eyes not leaving Brennan's face. 'A nerve poison used by the Fae a long time ago. I believed this knowledge had died. He will not live beyond tomorrow.'

With one swift slice, Carter pulled his arms back, watching the blades open the man's throat. Blood smothered him, and there was no noise as the half severed head lolled to the side.

'No. I will not accept that,' screamed Lilliana, her hand twisting again. Carter watched the last guard's neck start to implode on itself. Lilliana held her hand up, but turned her gaze to Brennan, 'Stand up, Brennan.' Her voice was strong, but saturated with despair. 'I order you. Soldier, stand up.'

'Lilliana. Stop,' said Cedric, cradling Brennan on his lap, 'This serves no purpose. Killing everyone is not the answer.'

'Tell me then, what is the answer?' Her eyes blazed tangerine, mixed with ferocious desperation.'

Cedric bowed his head knowingly. 'The Asrai are the only hope.'

Lilliana's head swam with a cold chill knowing the Asrai could never come here. They would have to move Brennan. The need for logic and action spilled through her, colliding with a sickening heat of dread that Brennan was dying.

'I will not lose him,' she screamed, and the words turned to a feral noise that hurtled down her chest, through her arm and out across the room towards the man who's fate was in her hand.

'Lilliana. Enough. Please.' pleaded Cedric. 'Killing another soul solves nothing. We are all as bad as each other.'

The man's eyes bulged against his cheekbones. His hands dropped to his sides, as his neck turned purple. The bones and cartilage that held his head up turned to dust inside his skin. Finally it was over.

Lilliana looked at Cedric. 'Their very heart beat is a threat. A promise to end us. My mother told me long ago, that power is not given to you... And so, I take it.'

*

Lorcan and Ava stood by the bodies of the Elders. Some looked burnt, some had fatal wounds to their heads. None had survived.

'The gateway is clear,' remarked Ava, 'Someone could have come through from Blair.'

'No,' replied Lorcan gently, bending to pick up a thin silver blade, engraved with dots and swirls similar to those across his back. 'No one has seen Lilliana since yesterday, and this,' he held it up for Ava, 'This is one of her knives.'

Lorcan's forehead crinkled with deep lines. His eyes burned, dark and dangerous. She thought about his hands on her last night and felt a heat spread down her body.

'I know telling you not to worry is pointless,' she said, taking his hand, 'But your sister is half goddess, and half hell. She looks like she may have won this fight.'

Lorcan closed his fingers around Ava's and placed her hand to his lips.

The wolves howled and circled them.

'You are part of their pack now,' he said, reaching down to touch the face of the largest black creature staring up at him with amber eyes. 'They will protect you, wherever you go. They will watch over you, as they do me.'

Ava reached out and the brown wolf ambled over to nuzzle against her hand. 'This one has been by my side for quite a while already,' she said, 'I think she knows more about us than she lets on.'

Lorcan kissed Ava's hand, and then brought his mouth down to hers. His lips caressed hers as he spoke quietly against her breath.

'I do not think I can live without you.'

Ava gently bit Lorcan's bottom lip, 'But what if I don't want to live in your big, stuffy castle?' she teased.

The black wolf sneezed and sat down by their feet.

'They mock me,' said Lorcan, smiling at his pack.

'Why?'

'Because they remember a time when they chased you through the forests of Blair. A time when I could have commanded the night, and them, to end your life.'

'That's charming. Really. Good to know.' Ava was smiling up at him, desperate to feel his lips on her again.

'In my defence I thought you were a danger to everything I believe.'

Ava pushed her hands up through Lorcan's hair, pulling his face towards her. 'And it looks like you were right,' she said, defiantly smiling as she kissed him.

*

Tabby's eyes had grown wider and wider as Foster had held on to her, begging her not to cry out. Not to reveal them. Now, as the final guard of The Order hit the floor, Tabby bit down on Foster's hand and bolted.

'Cedric,' she shouted running through the broken front door. 'Cedric, that can't be true.'

'Tabby?' exclaimed Carter, a moment of strange relief making him shiver. 'You're alive. You made it through. I looked everywhere,' and then he stopped talking. This was not the time. Never the time. 'Anyway, I'm glad you're OK,' he finished, stumbling awkwardly over the words and ignoring the surprised expression of Foster as he arrived.

'Everybody stop talking. Let's get Brennan to the gateway,' commanded Lilliana, the authority in her voice making everyone stare at her. 'Don't just stand there. If the Asrai are our only hope, that is where we are going.'

She wanted to hold Brennan. She wanted to weep and scream at the unfairness. But, there wasn't time. She would not admit defeat.

'And what if the Asrai won't help, Lilliana, or they tell us it's impossible. What then?' Cedric still had Brennan's head in his lap.

'You were once a great man in our land, Cedric. You, of all people, would never have given up.' Lilliana was desperate. And furious. 'You forged new Kings and taught the most dangerous sorcery of all. How can you sit there and tell me something is impossible? I do not know why you left the Kingdom, or why you let your only son believe you were dead, but now is the time to show him he is loved.'

'Cedric, you cannot leave us,' wailed Tabby, 'You have to stay. We need you. It's not true that Heath planned to poison us. It's just not true. He was a good man.'

Cedric bowed his head. A good man? Once, he had believed himself a good man. He had trained Kallan and

Heath to be strong leaders. He had equipped them with the tools to rule a kingdom... or destroy it. And for what? To be here now with his dying son in his arms?

'Who ever you are, little child,' replied Lilliana, staring at Tabby, 'Be quiet.'

'No,' retorted Tabby, looking at Foster for reassurance and then taking a step closer, 'Heath had a book. I saw him all the time. Writing stuff down. Drawing pictures. He told the others. He told the others if anything happened to him, to use the book. The book would save us.'

'Someone please make this child shut up.' Lilliana spoke, but didn't raise her voice. A small piece of her admired the guts and sass, but she couldn't care less about the people on this side. 'We don't have time for this,' she concluded, walking around Tabby and squaring up to Carter. 'I don't care if the people here live or die. I don't care what Heath was, or was not doing. I need Brennan moved and I need it done now.'

'There is room for both.' Cedric rose finally. 'And there is always room for humility, Lilliana.'

'So you'll help?' asked Tabby, her eyes wide and full of tears.

'Do you know where the book is?' Cedric's voice was calm, but Carter and Foster both noticed it crumple as he spoke. He looked more defeated than either had ever seen him.

'No. All he ever said, was that we'd find it close to his heart.'

There was a pause, everyone looked from one to the other. Carter knew the book wasn't on Heath when he killed him. He wondered what Tabby would think of him when she found out what he'd done.

'This is taking too long.' Lilliana's voice was fraught. 'Carter, help me with Brennan. I command you. You will bring him back to Daron with me.'

'What? How is that my responsibility?' replied Carter, wondering why he was even still standing with them all. 'I report to no one. You are not in charge of me.' He almost laughed. Asking would have been bad enough, but she actually thought she could order him about.

Lilliana raised her arm, flexing her fingers, 'If you don't help me...'

'Enough,' warned Cedric. 'I think I know where the answers may be. Annie's.'

Everybody stayed quiet, except for Lilliana, who tutted impatiently.

'I thought it strange at the time,' continued Cedric, 'But I didn't dwell on it. The trees. So many of them broken and torn. Roots upended. But there was one tree that remained alone.'

'That's a long shot?' questioned Foster.

'But it is all we have,' replied Cedric firmly. 'Doesn't it strike you as odd that Jess wrecked a path through from the cottage straight to Daron. That when she tore down without thought, she would leave one tree across her path. The perfect signpost that Strangers would ignore. Trees. Resilient, nurturing, cleansing, and, totally ignored by generations of Strangers.'

'Well I suppose when you put it like that.'

'Yes. Yes. Let's go,' yelled Tabby, now pulling at Foster's hand.

Lilliana raised an eyebrow. 'Well, you get on with that then. Good luck chasing your tails. Carter, you'll come with me.'

'I wish to come with you too, Lilliana,' said Cedric carefully. And then with a sigh that seemed heavy with loss, 'He is my son. I need to be with him.'

'But you said you would never set foot in Daron again?' Foster touched the old man's arm.

Cedric patted Foster's hand and smiled, but the edges of his mouth held no joy.

'Again with the orders, Lady Lilli.' Carter turned to leave the café. 'I'm not coming with you.'

Lilliana was about to stop Carter and demand he never call her Lilli again. He had no right, but Tabby got there first.

'My Gramme says the most miserable people are those that think only about themselves.' She paused, determined not to cry. 'But I'm not upset that you won't help us. I'm sad for you. Even the horrible lady over there is trying to help someone else.'

Carter would have laughed if the sight of Brennan were not so terrible. He looked at the little Fae's sad face, with eyes that still sparkled. He looked at Foster, broken, but holding Tabby's hand now. Pursing his lips, he exhaled like a spoilt child, scooped Brennan carefully into his arms and walked out the door.

Chapter 24

Cedric felt the rush of air as he stepped through into Daron. It smelt warm and sweet as it flooded his nostrils, but it chilled his bones. He kept the hood of his jacket up, even though he knew his presence would be recognised without the need to see his face.

The wolves bowed their heads and lowered their bodies to the ground. Ava spun round.

'Cedric.' She ran over to him, embracing him without hesitation.

'Daron suits you, my child,' he said kindly, pulling back to look at her face. He smiled at Lorcan.

'We are honoured to have you here.' Lorcan bowed his head slightly, placing his hand on Cedric's shoulder.

Cedric barely had time to look up at the turquoise sky, or acknowledge the huge Eagles swooping over head, when the whoosh of the gateway took everyone's attention.

'Lilli,' shouted Lorcan, surging forward. 'What were you doing?'

'Brennan?' interrupted Ava, pushing past Lorcan to reach Carter.

'He has been poisoned.' Cedric's voice was slow and weak. 'The venom of the cone snail. The Order have indeed been studying our ways.'

'Will he live?' Lorcan was asking Cedric, but glaring at Carter. How he wanted to rip out that man's heart where he stood.

Ava looked at Lilliana, and not for the first time felt common ground between them. For two people that refused to be friends, they had so much to fight for. She could see the pain in Lilliana's eyes, the set of her mouth determined not to give way to her feelings. To Ava, Brennan had become a friend, but she could almost reach out and touch the palpable misery streaming from Lorcan's sister.

'I don't know,' replied Cedric, the words catching in his throat, 'We need to take him to the waterfall, by the Forest of the Sith.'

'I'll start walking,' muttered Carter, adjusting the weight of Brennan in his arms, and stomping pointedly away. 'Anything but stand here and listen to your family reunion.'

'Asrai?' asked Ava.

'Yes,' replied Cedric, his eyes widening in recognition. 'You have come a long way, Ava,' he said, touching her arm gently. 'This is your world now, help shape it, or someone else will.'

'Perhaps she would be better off back in her own world.' Lilliana was keen to get moving and she couldn't bear any more fawning over Ava.

'Lilli.' Lorcan raised an eyebrow as he cautioned his sister.

'Wait,' said Cedric, raising his hand to quieten everyone. 'In this instance, Lilliana is right,' he counselled.

Lorcan and Ava stared as Cedric relayed the need to find out what Heath had been up to with The Order.

'I have to go back,' said Ava, already moving to the steps. 'I have to see Foster.'

'Good idea,' replied Lilliana, even though Ava wasn't addressing her. She was already moving away now, desperate to catch Carter up. 'Come on, Lorcan.'

'I am going with Ava,' he announced, surprised that his sister would think otherwise.

'What? That is a ludicrous idea. Why would you even consider it? What possible reason is there to want to help those people over your own?'

'You have Cedric.' Lorcan's voice was firm. He was already behind Ava, touching the small of her back to confirm his decision. 'And for what good he will do you, you have Carter. He is, at the very least, strong, and, it would appear, willing to help you. I too need to see Foster. He is my brother. And the Fae families in Blair are Ava's people.'

Lilliana scoffed and turned her back to Lorcan. She couldn't be sure, and she mulled it over as she rushed to catch Carter up, but she could have sworn she heard him add,

'And now, they are my people too.'

*

Foster stood staring at the carnage around Annie's cottage. He saw it with new eyes. About thirty paces from the front steps, in a direct line from the old wicker seats right through the forest - was a new path. Barely settled, the footprints of Jess's furore would last for a hundred years. But stood upright, almost gloating at the upended pines, was a Laburnum. Tall and healthy, it would bloom with highly scented vivid yellow flowers by May. But for now, it was enough that it stood firm.

'Toxic to the Strangers,' said Foster, touching the bark, wondering if Cedric might be right, 'But not to Fae.' He picked up the shovel he'd found in Annie's dilapidated shed.

'Or half Fae?' asked Tabby, looking at the ground around the base of the tree.

Foster smiled gently, 'I don't know,' he replied. 'Shall we dig?'

'There's a bit here.' Tabby pointed to the earth, 'A bit that looks nicer than the rest. Well, not nicer, but just a bit, I don't know.'

'Closer to Annie's heart?' suggested Foster.

Tabby stared at Foster. 'Foster, can I stay with you? Will you help me find Raz?'

Tabby's eyes filled with tears and Foster watched as she fought against her mouth, twisted with unheard sobs.

'What about your parents?' Foster tried to stop the words coming out his mouth, but his brain was not quick enough. A stupid thing to say, he knew it, but it was too late. Why else would she be asking? They must be dead.

'If they don't return, I mean,' she added quickly, not wanting to be a burden to him, 'I don't know where else to go.'

To Foster it felt like someone was holding his heart, pinching it with their fingers. Why must the innocent shoulder so much suffering? He squeezed Tabby's hand and thought about how he was no good for anyone. The only time he felt peace was in that second between sleep and awake. And then the world became an unbearable weight where he remembered he was balancing at the edge of madness. How could he possibly look after a child? How could he keep her safe? There was no way he was the best option. But he might be the only option. And, he wondered, looking at her now already digging with a small trowel, how could he ever leave her?

'Let's get this done first,' was all he said, wiping a stray tear before it fell, 'Let's see if our treasure is here.'

*

Carter placed Brennan down carefully inside the cave. The walls were high and the constant trickle of water an echoed tranquillity that filled the air with beads of cool moisture.

'Do we call the Asrai? What's supposed to happen now?' he asked Lilliana. He watched, irritated, as she smoothed her hand over Brennan's head.

As Cedric entered the cave the waterfall on the opposite

side of the cavernous drop sparkled with the shades of a fiery sunset.

'They know we are here,' he said plainly, nodding his head in reverence.

Carter looked around, wondering what Cedric saw.

'And will they come? Will they help?' Lilliana lifted Brennan's hand and pressed it to her face. She could hear his breathing, steady but shallow. She knew he could hear her. She held his fingers to her lips, so he could feel her too.

'I hope they have mercy on me,' said Cedric, but he was not looking at any of them. He stared at the falling water, a never ending formless force, carving new paths through the obstacle of the earth itself.

'A long time ago, you sentenced me to die.'

Lilliana and Carter stared towards Cedric, stunned at his words, but he didn't address them. He stared resolutely towards the water, and kept talking.

'No one Fae should have the power to life and death. I trained Kallan and Heath to know the endless rhythm of creation and destruction. I rejoiced in their efforts and I led them on a path of selfish glory. For a time, I forgot the majesty of this planet. You let me rule over it, and I foolishly decided I could dictate who lived and who died.'

Cedric paused, looking at Brennan. He knew if his son

could hear him, the words would cause pain. But, the time for protecting himself was finally over.

'I took life believing there would be no consequence. I thought only of the rewards the Fae craved. And I did not accept when it was my time to die.'

Carter and Lilliana watched transfixed as the waterfall undulated and foamed like an angry volcano.

'I know I have no reason to expect you to forge another deal with me. I left Daron, at your request, rather than face death. I vowed if I returned I would accept your punishment. And, in return, you have kept Daron safe. You should have been served by someone better than me.'

He couldn't look over to Brennan again, he knew he had to keep speaking. It mattered little what Carter or Lilliana thought of him. He only had the Asrai to answer to.

'But I learned. I changed. I have lived a simple life trying to serve others. To make amends. And I know now that life can never be eternal. But I also know that love is immortal. I am ready to die, I have come back to die. But, by your grace I ask one last thing. Death should be a distant rumour to my son. He does not deserve to pay along side me. I have torn away so many layers of myself, now all that is left is this truth. The truth of who I am. I am a father. I will gladly give my life to you, but ask with all the love of a father in my heart… please save my son.'

The water was like a lullaby to Brennan. He watched with half open eyes as Cedric bowed to the might of the Asrai's song. He closed them quickly when Cedric approached.

'It is my time. Please forgive me,' said Cedric gently, kissing his son's forehead, 'I did not give you much in life, so, please - let me have this.'

Brennan opened his eyes to watch his father walk away. He saw Carter turn and follow but could not catch the sound of his voice.

Only Lilliana remained. 'Do not leave me, Brennan,' she whispered against his lips. 'Do not make me mourn you.'

Brennan smiled at the touch of her mouth. 'Shut up and kiss me,' he murmured against her breath.

*

The book was bound with burgundy leather. Silk ribbons held all the loose papers inside from falling out.

'Close to Annie's heart,' repeated Foster.

'I told you there was a book.' Tabby sounded triumphant. She concentrated on stroking the wolf's back slowly. She had never been this close to them before, and now, finding herself sitting amongst them she felt very brave. She glanced up at Lorcan who was watching her intently, and then looked away quickly, deciding the wolves were less scary than he was.

Ava touched Foster's arm gently, 'Are you ready for this? We don't know what's in there.'

Foster wiped his hands down his legs, 'The pages look old, well used. Whatever he was doing it's not new. He was working on this for a long time.'

'While Annie… while our mother was still alive?'

'Looks that way. This book is worn.'

'You do believe he loved her, don't you?'

'Perhaps.'

'Foster, there is no way he would have had anything to do with Kallan taking you and treating you so badly.'

'We don't know that for sure. Sacrificing a half-Fae was a key to power. And our father's seemed intent on power.' He looked at Lorcan as he spoke. He craved the friendship they had once shared, and mourned it. How could they ever go back?

'You know power can corrupt even the best of us.' Lorcan spoke carefully.

'But not you, Lorcan,' whispered Foster, and he passed the book over, 'You read it, you tell us if Heath loved us - or used us.'

The wolves whimpered as two letters fell from the book.

Lorcan passed the first letter to Ava. 'It's from Grace,' he said softly, 'It should be you that reads it first.'

Ava started to read out loud.

Dear Heath

I am returning your letters, and your notebook. Please stop writing to me. As much as my heart sings to know you are alive, I cannot be part of this. I spent my life honouring the promise I made to Annie. I gave up planning a life for myself, to try and make the best life possible for Ava. Whilst it breaks my heart that you were unable to watch your children grow, you must understand that mine breaks at the very thought of you. I loved you, but you loved Annie. And even if you had loved me, I could never accept the magical ways I glimpsed. I dedicated my life to pretending none of it existed. My heart broke every time I saw how much Ava loved Annie, and I will not lie, and pretend the life she now has, is the life I wanted for her. I regret that I cannot stay in Blair and learn more about Foster. But I know enough from Cedric to know not to ask any more. I cannot bear the idea of his pain. From the moment Ava was in my arms I loved her as my own, and I would have loved Foster too. But I cannot deny I would have done anything to prevent them learning about their parents. So you see, I cannot be the keeper of any information, or your book. You must keep it buried close to your heart. I want nothing to do with it. But you must promise me you will keep Ava and Foster safe. At all costs, you must keep them safe. I hope that is what is in your heart Heath, but at the very least I expect you to honour Annie and do your duty.

My love for you will not fade, but these secrets are too many to keep.
Gracie xx

It was Foster that spoke first, 'So, she's not coming back?'

'It would appear not,' replied Ava, memories of Grace and Sean flooding over her. It all seemed so long ago, but just yesterday at the same time.

'I need to sit down,' she said flatly, dropping to the floor and allowing the wolves to nuzzle at her side.

Tabby smiled at her with a wide eyed innocence. 'You are like Raz, too,' she whispered, as if this was exciting news. 'We always told Raz he was the beauty of both.'

'Read the other letter,' instructed Foster to Lorcan, but it was Tabby he was watching. 'Please,' he added, not because of any duty he felt to Lorcan, but because Tabby had shot him a look that filled him with a sliver of shame.

Lorcan unfolded the piece of paper.

Dearest Grace,

You have not replied to my letters, but I fear I am running out of time. I hope at least you are reading them, and know how sorry I will always be for the pain I caused you. I hope it brings comfort, rather than more pain, for you to know that Annie was loved and I tried everything - to keep her from dying.

I wanted to hand you the enclosed book in person, for safe keeping, but now I have no time, and need to send it to you, along with knowledge that you must keep safe and, if the time comes, tell only Ava and Foster. I do not know who else to trust.

They may hear many stories about me, and to my shame, many of them will be true. But, please, make sure they know I spent years searching out the rarest plants, and animals in an attempt to make a medicine. I made deals with The Order for long forgotten incantations they had kept hidden. I tried all that was possible to stop Annie's life from fading. Perhaps walking away would have saved her, but she begged me not to. And I knew I never could. So our fate was sealed.

But there are others Grace. So many others. The medicine I made isn't perfect yet. I let The Order believe I am helping them to poison my own. And, indeed, I am dismayed as some of the children grow sick. So there is much work to do. The book contains the ingredients, and the ancient words, and should only be trusted to Ava or Foster. They may need Cedric's help, but I leave them to make that decision, if I am no longer here to make it with them. Tell them, I am convinced, when the magic is right, and the ingredients perfected, The Order will not be able to find the Fae. The medicine will make them undetectable. They will live in peace, wherever they choose. And the Stranger's that choose to love them, will not wither before their time is up. The medicine will keep them strong.

This, I believe, is the future for our kind. For centuries we relied on adoration to gain fertility and magic. Both sides always in conflict, and the slaughter of our own as a result. The Order believe the concoction will identify and poison Fae, but its purpose is to integrate.

Tell my children I thought of them every day. There is no word for a parent that loses a child. Such a piercing wound that never heals, there could be no word to explain it. I have no right to ask you to do any of this, but I ask anyway. I do not regret a single day of my time in your world. I wish you happiness Grace.

Heath.

Lorcan fell silent. He had chosen to be here with Ava and Foster, in Blair, but he felt so out of place. The world he had grown up in seemed more distant as each secret fell open. As if someone had made him look in a mirror his whole life, and suddenly this last year, the glass had broken and he was forced to look harder.

'See,' shouted Tabby, triumphant, and now brave enough to tickle the brown wolf behind the ear. 'I told you Heath was helping us.'

'Do you believe all this?' Foster asked Ava. It was a serious question. His brows were pushed together as he searched Ava's face.

'It makes sense, I suppose,' she replied, 'As much as anything makes sense. I mean, I hardly knew the real Annie, and we know nothing about Heath.' She looked at Tabby and couldn't help smiling kindly, 'I'm more inclined to believe what Tabby says. So. Yes. I think it's probably true.'

'Someone is coming,' interrupted Lorcan, stuffing the leather book down a pocket inside his coat.

'Bad men?' asked Tabby, cowering between two wolves.

'Yes. Probably,' replied Lorcan, 'Stay with the wolves.'

'Fae or Stranger?' Foster picked up the shovel.

Lorcan thought about what he'd just read. There was no denying that for some, on both sides, the idea joining Fae and Stranger was an extreme one, and not helpful to the play for power.

'That, is a good question,' replied Lorcan, glancing at Ava and then to Foster, and feeling the axis of his world shift.

*

Brennan laid still in Lilliana's lap. He could feel the rise and fall of her breathing. It soothed the burning racing through his body. He didn't think there was a cell that wasn't saturated with poison. He tried to focus on Lilliana's soft fingers tracing gently down his face.

'If I cannot be by your side,' he whispered, as the waterfall lulled her to sleep, 'I will not leave you. I will watch. I will watch, as you grow to become the Queen I know you will be.'

'Shut up, soldier,' she murmured, as she kissed each of his fingers and traced them across her smile. Her tears had soaked her lips, but she hoped he wouldn't notice. Lilliana had never been very good at waiting. She'd never had to wait for anything, but right now, as thunder cracked the sky outside the cave, she knew she would sit here forever if she had to.

*

Tabby counted six men. Five looking scraggy, and one at the back, tidy and smart. She slunk further into the wolf pack feeling the fur on each neck stand to attention. A low growl came from largest black wolf at the front as it stood next to Lorcan.

'We have no quarrel with you here today.' Lorcan spoke calmly, but his eyes had their usual poisonous glare.

'And yet you dare to come here, to our lands.' One man stepped forward, and Tabby noticed his hands and face were scarred as if no stranger to blades.

'We are just leaving,' replied Lorcan firmly, and he touched the wolf's head with his fingertips. The wolf glanced briefly up looking for instruction.

'Really,' said another, and he reached inside his jacket to remove a gun with a long barrel. 'Perhaps we don't want you to leave. Perhaps we just want you to die.'

Tabby watched as the tidy man at the back, made his way towards Lorcan. He smiled, but it was empty and cold. 'Why are you here?' he questioned, 'At this particular place? What could possibly be here for you?'

'There is nothing here,' answered Lorcan, 'We just came back for our friend.'

Tabby watched the man walk slowly around Lorcan. She thought he looked more elegant than the other men. It made him look more important. Like he didn't normally fight. Perhaps he gave out the orders. As he continued to walk, now deliberately aiming his gaze towards the hole in the ground, Lorcan crossed his arms and delved inside the long coat. He was careful to avoid Heath's book, pulling out long blades and spinning to face the man.

Everything happened in such a blur, that Tabby would never know who started it.

She saw Lorcan rush at the elegant man and slice the blades across his back hacking him down to the floor.

She heard his final words, spoken through a hostile grin, 'It does not matter how many of us you kill. You are doomed. We have your secrets. You have been betrayed by your own, and every last one of you will fall.'

Three were launching themselves towards Lorcan, their guns discharging a roar that made Tabby whimper.

'Ava,' he shouted, as he raised his blades towards their faces, 'Remember, you are part of their pack... be their leader.'

Ava and Tabby saw Lorcan fall. They saw his blood splatter the dirt. His face turned thunderous as pain coursed through him. 'Talk to them,' he yelled, as fury blazed from his eyes right through to the fingers that held the blades.

And then the wolves howled. A deep lasting noise that filled the air, made it feel solid, consumed everyone. Tabby looked at Ava and saw her eyes moving from each wolf to the next. She said nothing, but her lips talked. A dazzling light flashed from Ava. Tabby squinted and covered her face. Each wolf was glazed with it as the howling became loud and majestic.

Through her fingers, Tabby saw the wolves attack. The three men covering Lorcan had no chance to defend themselves. Tabby watched as the wolves with fur like velvet and tongues that had been tender and restrained, now shredded the flesh from Lorcan's assailants. At Ava's command they clawed and ruptured all three until blood covered everything and the air smelt of iron.

'Foster?' she asked tearfully, realising the last two men were approaching her.

'What you looking at?' one of them said, taking his eyes away from Tabby to where Foster was crouched. In his hands he held jewels the size of walnuts, each a different shade of darkest ruby, some almost purple.

'Give those to me.' The yell was dripping with greed. Tiny beads of saliva lined the man's lips as he surged forward.

'Tabby,' shouted Foster desperately, pulling himself up to grab at her.

The blades were so sharp, so noiseless, so effortless. Foster didn't feel them enter his chest. They had Fae blades. The thought flitted through his brain and then disappeared as he looked at Tabby's face. He knew then, they were connected by the exquisite metal.

They stared at each other. It was Tabby that smiled first. 'Don't let go of me Foster,' she whispered, as tears ran down her flawless cheek.

He hoped she didn't feel any pain. He wrapped his arms more tightly around her, willing her to feel peace as her life ebbed away.

'Never,' he replied gently.

*

Lilliana's breathing had slowed to a gentle rhythm. Brennan knew she was finally asleep. There wasn't much time left, but he'd made his decision hours ago. He clawed at the sandy earth, pinching it, as if trying to wake a sleeping beast. The waterfall, which had quietened to a steady pale lavender blur, foamed and started to sparkle with crystals of turquoise and emerald. He knew he had their attention.

'Do not take Cedric,' he whispered so quietly his lips hardly moved. He knew the Asrai heard, the water running down the walls of the cave fizzed in response.

'I do not want to leave,' he continued, closing his eyes for a second at the thought of Lilliana, 'But if someone has to die… Do not take Cedric.'

Brennan paused, knowing he did not have long before Lilliana heard the water hissing.

'If Daron, is to survive, its Fae need to grow, evolve, they need leadership as well as the strength of a warrior. A warrior who has known loss and defeat. Only through that loss will she know her strength. Only from her wounds will she learn to stand up. To hold herself together, when everyone expects her to fall apart. That will make her the true leader the Fae need. I know she is impossible, and she is argumentative, but to me, she is perfect. I do not wish this pain on her without regret, but you need to sacrifice me. My flesh and my heart need to fail, for my presence to give her strength.'

He felt weak now. He had no idea if the Asrai were really there. He would have laughed at how absurd he probably sounded, but his chest burned with venom. Did they really have the power to grant life and death? Perhaps Cedric's whole speech was for Lilliana's sake? To give her hope, where there was none? Had his father really been that powerful, here, in Daron?

'You need Cedric,' he muttered, before resting his head deeper into Lilliana's lap. 'Whatever peril the Stranger's realm faces, we have Fae there. They need his protection. Ava needs his help. There are new beginnings there, for our people and the Strangers. What happens there, will define us all.'

*

Tabby was only vaguely aware of the wolves as she and Foster fell backwards into the hole. She knew they had taken the final two men to the floor.

She tasted her own blood. She knew Foster had cushioned her fall as he hit the dirt, but she felt the sting of glass as their faces crushed the ruby jewels. She was covered in blood, so much blood, but it felt strangely cold.

Before she closed her eyes she saw Ava screaming silently towards the hole in the ground. Her eyes howled with misery and hopelessness. The air darkened as a bloodied, broken Lorcan pulled at Ava's arm to stop her climbing down to where they lay. She saw Ava surge round to struggle and punch against Lorcan.

And all the while, in her head, she could hear Foster. He soothed her with his words.

'You and I are in this together, Tabby. Do not give up yet. The end is not the answer.'

*

Lilliana woke up shivering. She had no idea how long they had been in the cave. The water ran down the walls subdued and balmy. She stroked Brennan's face.

A tight pinching scream heaved up from her stomach and blasted at the waterfall.

'You took him.' There was no anger in her voice, just utter agony.

The volume of torment tore around her, the water surged and frothed in response.

'You took him.'

Hours passed.

Hours, where she simply held Brennan's head on her lap and wept.

'You took him from me.'

'After everything. You took him from me.'

The Asrai cried with her. The poison had done too much damage. Lilliana was blind to their tears. Her misery and growing rage colouring the air around her.

At the edges of the cave, the creatures of Daron and the Forest of the Sith stayed silent and listened.

'You took him from me.'

And then, a new dawn, and a new Queen emerged.

'I will never forgive you, Asrai. I will never forgive, and I will never forget how this moment feels.'

Chapter 25

Christmas overtook Blair. Just like the previous year, for those in the new quarters of town, the glare of electric fairy lights drowned out the stars. Here, at Annie's cottage, time stood still. The ground was hard with a winter frost that couldn't be melted by the weak December sun. The damage Jess had done was iced with white. Ava knew when the spring came the animals would trample through it and spread new life, but for now she was content that Jess felt close. She had made her mark. A whole year, thought Ava, a whole year ago and she and Jess had been normal young women. None of this had existed.

Except it did exist. It had always existed.

Ava turned her attention back to the tree. The tree that Jess had saved. The tree that held all the secrets. She had decided to call it the Salvos tree.

The Survivor Tree.

Pagans would have brought a tree into the house, so the wood spirits would be kept warm during the cold winter months. But this tree was too special to ever cut down. Ava felt sure it would blossom in the spring, and she hoped it would bear fruit every year. In winter though, that would be their special time. She planned to hang food and treats on the branches every Christmas. She smiled, knowing the others would say they were gifts for the spirits, but it was enough for her to know the animals would leave their warm forest and visit her. She would hang bells on the branches so the 'appreciative spirits', and the squirrels, could say thank you.

'Would you like my help?'

Lorcan's breath was on her neck as he spoke. She shivered.

'How long have you been there?' she laughed, wondering why she never heard his approach.

'Long enough to know you need help.' His voice held humour, and it warmed Ava.

'Well, I don't.' She smiled, turning round. 'Unless you've come to kiss me?'

His eyes found hers. They stared with more intimacy than

any words. And then his mouth was on her. As the kiss deepened, Ava felt heat blister its way through her body.

They both smiled at the same time, breaking the kiss, when a wolf playfully forced his head between them, pushing their bodies apart. Ava reached down and ruffled the ginger patch of fur between his ears.

'There is room for everyone,' said Lorcan, crouching down to kiss the wolf gently.

'Is there?' said Ava, feeling the moment of joy fade, 'Do you think she'll come?'

'I can only hope,' he replied seriously, gently tracing his finger around the wolf's ear. 'Lilli has always been strong willed, and, she probably likes this world even less than before. But, I remain with hope.'

Lorcan had tried to enter Daron several times in the last few weeks, but Lilliana had guards crowded around the Oak tree. Day, and night, they refused exit and entry. They knew who he was, but her orders were final. No one could leave or enter until she said so.

'Be gentle with her if she comes today. It will be very difficult for her. I can't imagine her pain. I didn't realise how close they'd become. It was so unlike your sister. And now, she must feel pure misery.' Ava choked out the last few words. She had lost too many people in the last year. A wave of sorrow threatened to floor her. She would always miss Brennan.

'Do you know what the Asrai would have done with his body?' She almost didn't ask, the words clawed at her heart. No chance to ever say goodbye. 'Would seem they have a habit of choosing who lives, and who dies.'

'No,' he replied simply, standing up and pressing his lips to her forehead. 'I cannot imagine losing you, Ava. The thought of it tears at me.' He felt the stab of his secret digging at his stomach. What would Ava do, if she found out it was him who had killed Jess, and not the Asrai?

'What?' Ava looked up into Lorcan's face. 'Where did that come from? Why would you lose me?'

'I am struggling with this new concept of uncertainty,' he sighed, trying to sound light, 'That is all.'

So formal, thought Ava. So afraid to show his feelings still. 'Well,' she said, handing him a fistful of treats for the Robins and Goldfinch, 'I've heard Cedric say that uncertainty is the energy of life.'

While Ava was thinking what else she could say to keep Lorcan from brooding, a mob of deer crunched out from the forest, diverting them both to the tree line.

'What could you possibly have to tell me, brother, that requires me to come back to this awful place?' Lilliana stood firm at the edge of the Pines. She had never seen the cottage before, but the memories that Blair held for her were as bitter as they were sweet. 'Get it over with.' The deer tilted their heads to watch Lilliana as she surveyed the land around her. She was wearing a long fur, but underneath she was dressed in body hugging suede and looked ready for battle.

'I would have come to Daron, but you prevent passage,' he replied, touching the wolf gently to quiet its unease. In truth, he had enjoyed the time in Blair, with Ava, more than he had imagined possible. 'I have decided there should be no secrets between us all. That has to end.'

Lilliana's lips lifted at the irony of Lorcan's words. She had very little to keep secret while he, she doubted, had told Ava the truth about Jess's death. And then she looked at the baubles Lorcan still held and she shook her head, blinking slowly. 'Well, aren't you just the darling of the Strangers. Tell me Lorcan, are we going to be one big happy family?'

'Why can we not try that?' interrupted Ava, already wishing she hadn't planned the gathering.

'Once again I find myself thanking you,' she said addressing Ava, but disregarding the question, 'You saved my brother from The Order, or rather the wolves did. And for that I am grateful.' There was a pause before she added, 'However, it pains me to know you can now command the wolves, and I sincerely hope you do not have plans to increase your power.'

Footsteps behind Lilliana made her sigh, and raise her eyebrows. 'I hope you don't mind,' she said mischievously, as Carter stopped by her side, 'I brought a guest.'

Ava grabbed Lorcan's arm and pulled him back. His eyes blazed and she could see a vein pulsing on the side of his neck.

'Why would you trust him, Lilli? After everything he has done. Why him?'

'Trust!' Lilliana wanted to laugh. That was the last thing on her mind. 'You think I trust anyone anymore? As long as Carter is useful, he is welcome in Daron.'

'Useful?' repeated Lorcan, raising an eyebrow, 'And how exactly could he be useful to you? Your whole life you have dismissed the Strangers and now you make friends with one of them?'

'Hey.' interrupted Carter, 'Let us not forget I have Fae blood too. The best of both worlds.' He had meant to sound upbeat. He had been determined not to be the outsider today, but his words reminded him of Tabby.

'I have been underestimated my whole life,' continued Lilliana, 'Carter has knowledge. Other realms. Other Fae. The Strangers. The Order. Shall I go on? And while the Elders watch me, and talk about me, and think they will manipulate me, I listen, I learn. I will rule and I will rule well. I will rule to my own terms - and I will love on my own terms.' The last words started to crumble as they left her lips, a flash of Brennan consumed her, but she cleared her throat and stared defiantly at Lorcan. 'Carter has agreed to stay. For as long as I deem it necessary.'

Lorcan was about to say, I bet he has, but Lilliana cut across him,

'Besides, there is no one better to amuse our mother. He can be quite charming when he wishes.'

'At least you have your mother,' mumbled Ava. She was starting to fidget and wanted to get to the point of the gathering. They had important information Lorcan needed to share with Lilliana, and now Ava just wanted it over with.

'How interesting that you judge me.' Lilliana's voice was steady, but everyone knew it was laced with outrage. 'Since my brother met you, all you have done is sulk about being lied to by the women who raised you. By Annie, and, by Grace. You think you were betrayed. You believe you deserved better. Whine. Whine. Whine.' She stopped to take a breath. She would not allow Ava to see the hurt. She bit her lip, and breathed again, deeper this time. 'But in fact, everything they did for you, they did quietly out of love. They protected you. They tried to keep anyone from ever hurting you. Whereas me, Ava, I was going to be betrayed all along. I have a mother who has told me she loved me my entire life, but in truth, her actions have been quite the opposite. She will always love power and herself, more than she loves being a mother. And given the choice she will take betrayal every single time. Even now, while I am here, she meets with the Elders in secret, believing that she is better placed to rule than I am.'

'Well then, we have something to show you that will give you an edge. Information she will never get hold of.' Ava was outraged, but she could hear the distress in Lilliana's voice. If they had been friends she might have put her arms around her, told her to cry. Maybe, one day, she thought to herself. But for now, she would help Lilli stand tall. Today was not the day to make Lorcan's sister the enemy.

Lorcan held out a piece of paper to his sister. 'Read this, and then we will show you.'

As Lilliana started to read, Lorcan added quickly, 'It was a page inside Heath's book. The book he'd buried by the tree. We didn't find it until… well read it, and then you'll see.'

I am writing this down, although I have shared it with no one. I can scarce believe any of this could be true. The idea that a Stranger who helps the Fae could be brought back from the dead by the waters of Daron's lake, was myth so old it was inconceivable that it was real. But in archives of The Order were legends stolen from the Fae. Legends where we can dare to hope that it is true - Creation is the only noise louder than destruction.

Jess consented to give me samples of her blood. Nobody knows I asked her. It is too important and needs to be kept secret. The legends say her blood holds the key to a time of peace. A time of unity. She knows helping me will weaken her, and shorten the new life she has been given. But she also knows that she cannot last in this form. There is too much at stake for any force on this earth to let her live in peace. She herself will not be able to contain the power she holds. So, she chooses to help in the hope she will be remembered well.

There is much work to do and I fear I will need to spin tales to both sides to be allowed to work unhindered. I could not save Annie from loving me. I could not heal the ailments that drained her life. But I may be able to save others. And I may be able to hide the Fae from detection in the world of Strangers. I want to create a way for Fae and Strangers to love together, and live in peace. This may be the only way forward for the continuation of the Fae. The alternative is to hunt each other down as we have done for generations.

Hate breeding hate, until no one remembers to live. I do not know if it will work, or how much time Jess and I have to work on this. If someone else is reading this, it is probable that time ran out.

Lilliana looked up from the paper and stared at Ava, and then Lorcan.

'They fell, you see,' started Ava, 'Foster, and Tabby. They fell back into the hole we had dug, and Foster was holding what he thought were jewels.'

Everyone stared as Tabby came slowly out on to the porch. Her eyes peeped out shyly from under a mass of curls. She dragged Foster by the hand.

'But it wasn't jewels in his hands. It was vials. Of blood. Jess's blood. The glass broke, the blood entered their wounds.'

'He didn't die,' muttered Lilliana, and her eyes filled with tears at the sight of Foster. A long shiver stole through her as she stared, feeling the empty sickness again that Brennan was gone.

'Jess got to be the hero she always wanted to be – again,' said Foster, smiling at Lilliana. She smiled back, wanting to rejoice, but fighting a weight of sadness. She took deep breaths to steady the overwhelming urge to collapse to the ground.

Foster took her hands and squeezed them gently. 'Lilli, we all have another chance. Look around, at all of us. Each of us broken, and each has a chance to be beautiful, to carry the realms forward on our shoulders. But not like a burden. Like wings.'

Carter wasn't listening. He surged forward and scooped Tabby in his arms. He hadn't stopped to think about why, he just felt a balmy reprieve rush through his body.

'You're squashing me,' she giggled, the timid expression replaced by one Carter recognised.

'There is much to do,' said Lorcan, bringing a sense of foreboding to the scene. 'We have to work out which point Heath reached with his medicines. We need to gather more supplies of hornbeam and cherry plum from the Sith. Some of the children, Fae and half-Fae remain sick. And we do not know much, yet, about Jess's blood. We do not know why it healed.' He stopped talking, aware everyone was staring.

Tabby rolled her eyes. 'I'm glad you're here,' she whispered to Carter. 'Lorcan is so serious. He scares me more than the wolves.' She smirked at Lorcan as she spoke, and Carter couldn't help laughing out loud.

'None of this is my business,' said Lilliana. 'I don't care about the people here. I cannot force them to return to Daron, but I will not condone or assist in this ridiculous notion of everyone living happily ever after. This is not my problem, I have enough of my own to return to.'

'Actually, Lilli, it *is* your problem too.' Foster kept hold of her hands. 'The Order are not stupid. Just as Heath was double crossing them, they may well have been planning the same. What if the medicine just creates an addiction? The Order may have the recipe to spread an addiction through the realms, give themselves power over generations to come. Fae everywhere could be at risk, not just here.'

'What is it you expect me to do?' Lilliana took a step back from Foster. His words sounded wise, but they also sounded like Cedric.

'At the very least, to begin with, grant us passage through Daron to The Forest of the Sith,' said Ava. She was talking to Lilliana, but her eyes were focussed on Carter and Tabby. 'The plants that Toni needs to cure the sickness are there. It's a start.'

'But no one must know,' cautioned Lorcan, 'We must have a bond between us. We must all promise to keep this to ourselves. There are extreme views amongst some Fae, and Strangers.'

Lilliana thought about The Elders at home, waiting to marry her off. She would certainly not be telling them about today.

'Cedric believes this may be a way for the Fae to return to fertility. Not everyone will embrace the idea. They will see it as diluting both sides. Some Fae will never agree to giving up devotion, some Strangers will never agree to give up religions that only benefit their wealth. But over time, we may have discovered a way for those who choose it, to live together in peace.'

'I will help you where I can,' stated Lilliana, pulling the fur around her, making ready to leave. 'But do not mention Cedric's name to me. He is not welcome in Daron.'

'Try to be kind, Lilli. He lost too.'

Lilliana shot a look at Lorcan, but said nothing to him.

'Are you coming, Carter? Or are you staying to play with your friend?' Her words were playful, but she didn't meet Tabby's gaze, she stared only at Carter.

Lorcan raised an eyebrow, that his sister could pick and choose when to be kind. Tabby noticed a softness in the way Carter looked at Lilliana, and she wrapped her arms around him tightly.

'I am coming with you,' she sang, 'I can make you smile when your friend with the fiery hair is grumpy with you.'

'Oh joy,' said Lilliana, looking at Tabby with disdain.

'She reminds me of you, when we were little,' smiled Foster.

Lilliana arched one perfect brow.

'You're coming too, silly,' remarked Tabby, and she pulled Carter by the hand to where Foster stood. Lilliana smirked at the sight. Tabby grinning holding hands with both Foster and Carter.

'The three of you? You surely cannot be serious?' Lilliana hands went to her hips.

'Why not? I'm going where they go?' Tabby looked

fearlessly at Lilliana, copying her stance.

'Like I said, Lilli, reminds me of you when we were little. Besides, I think I will go where Tabby goes.' Foster winked down at the little girl, 'I'm not sure Carter is the right role model.' He wondered how he would learn to live again, but he knew life had a habit of carrying on. He wasn't ready to face the guilt if joy returned, but he knew, as he looked at Tabby, he had to find a way to live with himself. 'There is more for me in Daron, than here. For the time being, at least, this place holds too much pain.'

He was aware everyone was looking at him, and he couldn't stand their pity. He pushed his shoulders back and turned to Carter.

'At least this way Tabby won't be on her own, when you get bored and decide to meddle.'

Carter was about to reply, but Lorcan beat him to it.

'How does it feel, Carter?' he asked, his voice cutting with irony, 'You helped to bring Jess back, thinking you would have a weapon to use against everyone. You wanted to destroy any harmony that endured. But you may have done something noble instead. You may yet be part of reconciliation and new beginnings.'

He waited, expecting sarcasm. Wanting a witty response that would cause him anger. Desperate for a reason to lash out at Carter.

But Carter just smiled at Tabby, 'Funny how things work

out, Lorcan. I'd normally love to stay and argue, but I've got more important things to do.'

*

Lilliana had reached the arch when she spotted him, waiting. She wondered if he meant to approach Foster and Carter walking behind her, but it was her he stepped in front of.

'You must think yourself someone very special indeed, old man,' she said, with no trace of kindness in her voice. 'Let me pass, for there is nothing you could have to say, that I would want to hear.'

'I understand,' he replied softly. He looked crumpled, as if one shot of power from Lilliana's fingers would floor him. 'And yet, I hope you will listen to my words.'

'Let him speak Lilli.' Foster touched her arm gently, 'It was not his wish to lose Brennan.'

Lilliana said nothing, but she stood still, facing Cedric.

'I had no desire to cause you pain, Lilliana. I cannot fathom why the Asrai would take my son, and save me. This is the part of my story, where I am supposed to die. But now my existence has been forever changed. As has yours. And we will need to bear it with strength or the loss will be for nothing.'

The flash of hidden pain that lit Cedric's eyes as he spoke was haunting. Lilliana knew that pain. She felt it ripping at the muscles around her heart. Twisting and pinching her until she couldn't breathe.

'You will survive,' he continued. He would have reached out to touch her hand, but he knew that was expecting to much. 'Because the fire inside you, Lilliana, burns brighter than any fire around you ever will.'

'Have you finished?' Lilliana knew Cedric was right. His words hurt, but that didn't mean they were wrong.

'The Elders will expect you to be weak now. They will try to control you. But your people will see your scars. Let them know you are scarred, and all the stronger for it.'

His voice trembled as he spoke, a mixture of grief and admiration for the young woman who stood before him looking defiant behind her sorrow.

'Some days,' she muttered towards the floor, not knowing why she was speaking, 'The grief is so painful, I cannot move.'

Cedric felt the truth in every word.

Lilliana remembered her own words to the people of Daron...

'A leader earns her serenity… Time must, and will, test her… She will not have admiration simply bestowed on her, as a right of birth… I will suffer, and I will grow more beautiful each day because of our suffering.'

They were Brennan's words, as much as they were hers.

Cedric nodded to Foster and Carter before taking a step back. He would not push himself closer to Lilliana, not until she was ready. Tabby smiled at him, and he felt small comfort that Lilliana didn't know it yet, but she had the people she would need by her side.

'I do thank you for your words, Cedric,' she offered politely, blinking hard to steady herself. Brennan would be furious if she did not show his father some courtesy. 'Your advice will be heeded, and Daron will survive for another thousand years.'

Cedric could see her eyes blaze like a tiger as she spoke, but he knew he was not forgiven.

As Lilliana walked to the arch, she knew the words she wanted to say. In her heart she knew Cedric would always be on her side. But it was easier, as it had been all her life, to lash out at kindness. Push it away and pretend she didn't need help. Dismiss it now. Do the hurting, before someone hurts you first.

'But know this, old man.' She couldn't make eye contact with him. 'You made your choices a long time ago. And even if the Asrai have forgiven you, I cannot. You are not welcome in Daron. Your advice will not be sought by me, ever again.'

Chapter 26

Ava sat under the Salvos tree watching the stars through the bare branches.

'The sky looks the colour of figs tonight,' she remarked to Toni and Cedric as they sipped on hot chocolate.

'I know,' Toni replied, looking relaxed, 'It makes the moon look lilac. Perhaps a little piece of Daron's sky has come to watch over us.'

She sighed. The last few weeks had been busy. And come the new year, the work would start again.

Cedric remained quiet, sipping at the mug in his hands. He

and Toni had not faltered in their efforts to help the local Fae, and half-Fae, in Blair, but so far they had only seen small successes. Still, he mused, that was progress. He was determined to keep the work discreet. He wanted to stay in the shadows. His presence had become too noisy, too visible over the last year and it had brought them all too much loss. Brought him too much suffering. Like the Asrai, he knew it was better to hide in deep silent water, than flit noisily around the shallow.

'We are running low on medicine,' remarked Toni, saying her thoughts out loud. 'And the remainder of Jess's blood is running low.' She looked at Cedric, before turning to Ava. 'We hate to ask, but, do you think Tabby would give us more blood? It's more successful than Foster's. It seems you were right that she is the key now. Perhaps she absorbed more from the original vials. We don't ask lightly, we know she is so young.'

'I will go.' The voice boomed from nowhere, as usual, and Ava jumped.

'Do not expect me to apologise for my entry.' Lorcan raised his eyebrows as he watched Ava wipe the chocolate that had spilt down her chin. 'If you had not given the wolves those blankets, they would be by my side.'

Toni laughed. 'They certainly have made themselves at home,' she said, looking at the cottage porch where six wolves curled on quilted blankets.

'It was Tabby's idea, not mine.' Ava smiled. 'Annie would have loved it,' she added. Ava knew if she asked them, the wolves would now run to her side with the quietest command. As if on queue, the wolf with the ginger between his ears stretched and rolled onto his back.

'Thank you, Lorcan. And more plants for the medicine please,' said Toni, picking up the conversation. 'How was your sister last time you went through?'

'The usual,' he replied, 'It is best to love her, but leave her to be wild. She will steal the stars before she admits we are all in this together.'

'And yet she helps us?' Ava took Lorcan's hand as she spoke, and he raised it to his lips.

'Yes. She will rule her own way,' sighed Lorcan, 'And like the Salvos tree, I hope the branches will grow in different directions, but the roots will keep us as one.'

'With Kallan and Heath both dead, the daughters have ascended. And they will need to find a path - to exist together - in a way their fathers never could.'

It was Cedric that had spoken and everyone looked at him, as he had been so quiet. 'It will be imperative to everyone's survival. And she will bear her pain with courage,' he added, 'But Lilli's greatest battle, when the pain subsides, will always be her pride.'

Lorcan looked at the cottage, and the tree, and then Ava. 'Cedric, did you not tell Ava that this world is now hers to shape?'

'Yes. I did,' replied Cedric, the hint of a smile touching his lips.

'To shape, before someone else does,' repeated Lorcan. 'If we are successful, a new, strong community will evolve here. But the fight won't go away. And it won't be against each other any more. There will be unknown, middle ground, for both sides to fight over. There is always someone that wants to fight.'

'Do you miss it?' Ava asked Lorcan, 'When you go back to Daron, do you wish you could stay there?'

'Sometimes,' he replied, but his inky eyes burned with love, 'Only sometimes. But Jess left you a legacy Ava. She is the beginning, not an ending.'

*

It was late when Ava watched Lorcan return across the clearing, striding towards the porch. Most of the wolves had stayed with her. Only the black one ambled by his side. He had walked Toni and Cedric home, but Ava waited for his return never quite able to shake the dread that he might not come back.

As she watched him, she thought back to Annie and the story of the man she now knew had been her father.

'He was tall. His long coat billowed out behind him over a pure white crumpled shirt, that he wore like a messy schoolboy. His hair was like ink, falling about his face untamed. And his eyes...oh his eyes were like poison, Ava. And then he bowed.... A slow deliberate bend, but his eyes wouldn't release me. And when he finally spoke... every creature in the forest fell silent and let his words weave themselves into every thread of their being.'

The story that had consumed her then, was now her story too. The life she had hated, imprisoned by rules and convention was gone.

Slowly, Lorcan bent down and placed his lips against her neck. She felt the familiar warmth of his touch move through her body.

'The cottage may never be as comfortable as your castle,' she whispered as his lips grazed her throat.

'I do not want my castle,' he said, pulling back, staring at her with an intensity that made her breathing shallow, 'I only want you. When you kiss me, it is as if only that keeps me alive. So wherever you are, Daughter of Daron, is a battle worth fighting. By your side, will always be my home.'

...End

Other titles by Jane Dare

Wearing Pink Pyjamas

Telling people they're equal, isn't enough to make it so. Set across the late 1980's and through the 90's, follow the entwined lives of three women who have grown up with a promise of equality and freedom of choice. For them, though, the world is still shadowed by inequity and they must find the tenacity and vision to succeed despite the shady underbelly of life that exists beyond the edge of acceptable.

Vivacious and beautiful, Kitty hadn't planned what to do with life when an assault by a trusted family friend leaves her violated and afraid. As one by one every man she has ever loved lets her down, the struggle to find a path back to normal edges further out of her reach.
Bee is unashamedly planning a life filled with an immaculate home, a handsome husband and perfect children. When she meets Bob, an accomplished antique dealer, she's content to waltz blissfully through the opulent life he offers.
A village upbringing makes Angela burn with determination to escape and forge her own impression on the world. But ambition can be blind. Will her drive to prove she is better than her beginnings leave a path of heartbreak for Angela with no way back?

Set against a background of hidden organised abuse and a rapidly flourishing drug trade this is a story of love, loss, success and sacrifice.

Daughters of Daron – The Lost Daughter

Annie lived her short life blessed, and cursed, by a powerful love that came to her in the space that exists between awake and sleep. In her woodland cottage, it was intense and beautiful and ... enough. But now someone dares to reach beyond desire and the power of illusion. Ava, consumed by her Aunt Annie's stories of love and longing, starts to uncover the secrets binding them all together. As the world she knows unravels, and the beautiful strangers she meets become more dangerous, she will take you to a place full of fury, passion and vengeance. No one is who you think they are and everything has a price.
Will you follow Ava into the woods?

You can connect with Jane on Facebook - Jane Dare / Wearing Pink Pyjamas or follow her on twitter at www.twitter.com/ladybholaj

Jane's blog can be found at wearingpinkpyjamas.wordpress.com

Special thanks to Stephanie Parcus for her amazing cover design www.stephanieparcus.com

Printed in Great Britain
by Amazon